The Murder Hobbyist

A Brown & McNeil Mystery
Frank Lazarus

Frank Lazarus

Copyright

The Murder Hobbyist
Copyright Frank Lazarus © 2025
Published by Frank Lazarus
All rights reserved.

No part of this publication may be reproduced or distributed in print or electronic form without prior permission from the author.

No part of this book has been written by Artificial Intelligence.

This is a work of fiction. Names, characters, places, and incidents are products of the author's imagination or **used fictitiously.** Any resemblance to actual events, locales, or persons, living or dead, is entirely coincidental.

I am glad to accommodate those readers who have requested a larger type size.

To fellow authors, editors, and English Professors: I have noticed that I write like I think, often imperfect in structure but understandable. Following many discussions with my editor, I stayed true to myself. I hope you can bear with the imperfections. FL

Books by FL

The Murder Gambit (*)
The Phenom (*)
Recruiting Murder (*)
April Fools, Volume One: The Candidate (*)
April Fools, Volume Two: Claudia's Revenge (*)
103 First Dates: MisMatchDotCom
Is Anything Alright?
The Murder Hobbyist (*)
Brown and McNeil, The Beginning (Novella *)
The First Twenty Dates (Novella)
April Fools: The Candidate (Novella *)

(* Brown & McNeil Mystery Series)

PROLOGUE

My name is Frank Lazarus

Some background...

I am seventy-eight years old. I grew up in West Philadelphia and attended public schools.

After graduating high school, I joined the army for two years before attending St. Joseph's University while working.

I spent fifty-three years in the Life Insurance and Financial Services industry accumulating two ex-wives, three children, and five grandchildren.

Since my retirement at the end of 2021, I have become a self-published author. To date, I've published six books: five Brown & McNeil Murder Mystery novels and one work of creative nonfiction, *103 First Dates: MisMatchDotCom*, detailing my dating experiences from 2006 to 2013. It wasn't pretty.

Having read and written extensively on the subject, I felt I had become quite knowledgeable in murder, investigations, law enforcement, arms, and similar topics.

To my utter surprise, I shockingly decide to commit murder.

I go into murder mode.

I'm on a roll. Taking my readers along for the ride, I can make this my second Creative Non-Fiction book.

One thing; you need to promise not to tell. I don't plan on getting caught. If you feel this is too much to ask, PLEASE STOP READING NOW!

If you're still here, let's begin the journey.

Chapter 1

Deciding to kill someone is a HUGE!
WHOM to kill has to be a very close second.

It should be someone you hate a lot. But other than Donald Trump and his gang of trumpnuts, I don't hate anyone that much. I'm not planning to kill Trump. My luck I'd only nick him in the ear, and who wants all the attention that would bring? I move on to the immensely disliked candidates and there are many more options here.

I need to decide WHERE to kill someone. I spend most of my time on Hilton Head Island, South Carolina. The people I'm acquainted with in this area live in my apartment building. I mildly dislike a couple of them, but do they reach the level of murder candidates? I'll need to think about that.

But I spent most of my life in Philadelphia, and plenty of options exist there. The added plus for Philly, it gives me the added advantage of returning to Hilton Head, removing myself as a suspect unless I leave evidence, which I don't plan to do.

The who and the where are intertwined. I'll do it wherever my intended victim lives.

I narrow my focus to family members, former friends, neighbors, past co-workers, and people I don't even know that piss me off. This last group could include restaurant servers, mailmen, co-tenants in the office buildings, the owner of the food cart, and the guy who rides on your train every day; you get the idea.

The upside of picking someone from this group is the police always start by asking who wanted this man dead. They'll never have me in mind.

There are always ex-wives or women who rejected me. A few candidates might come to mind if you read *103 First Dates: MisMatchDotCom*.

But I find killing a man much more appealing. There is something too cowardly about killing a woman: it sounds sexist, but I consider it as gentlemanly.

This is not a decision I approach without careful consideration, nor do I wish to rush into it. The worst thing that could happen would be to kill Harry, get home, and think, *oh shit, I should have wacked Billy.*

This may shock many of you, but I am not considering anyone in my family. I mean, my parents, aunts, uncles, and even first cousins are all deceased.

My kids, grandchildren, and brother Rob are all good people, and I hope they will have long and happy lives.

Tawana could be a candidate, but after nine months of dating, it's too soon to tell.

I need to digress for a second.

I have given little thought if I should share this murder plan with anyone. Too many things can go wrong. They might not like who I selected as the victim or worse, try to talk me out of it as if this were some whim. I'm not telling anyone, at least until the cops are dragging me out in cuffs.

Thanks for bearing with me. Talking this out with you has helped, and I keep coming back to one name: Sean O'Connor. He's perfect. No one will miss him. Some will thank me in their prayers. Others may want to know why I waited so long.

He has not improved in the last thirty years.

Chapter 2

What's so special about this Sean O'Connor? Fair question!

O'Connor must be seventy-three years old by now. He is probably retired, still cheating on his wife, and estranged from his gay son.

I have not seen or heard from him in over ten years, although I read about him in the Inquirer. He attended a charitable event or received an award from a group for a large contribution.

I am not a religious guy, but is it true in some religions, you can buy your way out of hell? It would leave me in hell with a bunch of other poor folks. And how much would it cost to get elevated to the Pearly Gates?

It might be obvious; O'Connor is filthy rich. How rich must one be to be considered *filthy rich?* It's not important to my story, but I'm curious.

You might expect to learn the life story of Sean O'Connor.

Sorry! I'll share what I know, but it's not like I can call him and say, "Hey, Sean, I'm writing a book on how I'm going to kill you. I need some backstory on you. You know, how you became such an asshole, etc. Can you give me an hour?"

He grew up in Gladwyne, a ritzy suburb west of Philadelphia. Passing up more convenient private schools like Devon Prep and Malvern Prep, Sean attended Saint Joseph's Preparatory School in North Philadelphia. To anyone who attended or had a father or grandfather who attended, it is better known simply as *The Prep*.

After that, he got an accounting degree from Immaculata, and then an MBA in Finance at Wharton.

After working for a small accounting firm in the city for five years, he started his own Wealth Management Firm, The O'Connor Group, in 1978.

Giving credit where I must, O'Connor showed vision, and rather quickly, The Group comprised accounting, investment, and insurance divisions.

The financial services industry was breaking down the barriers that had kept those disciplines separated for the past hundred years.

I joined the firm in 1985 as the Vice President of The O'Connor Insurance Group.

Chapter 3

With hindsight, perhaps I should have known that O'Connor and I would mix like water and oil.

I recall that, during the interviews, he held his cards close to his vest. He shared little about his vision for the life insurance division. That was my area of expertise.

Other divisions specialized in Property and Casualty Insurance, and Employee Benefits. He felt that a customer of one division would become a customer of all divisions. O'Connor was unaware of how to bring that about. "You guys are the experts; figure it out."

All the clients were affluent, if not wealthy. There was an expectation that a new client would meet a minimum annual income and/or a net worth of five million dollars. Small to medium-sized business owners, doctors, lawyers, and other professionals comprised potential clients of the firm.

With O'Connor delegating, the five-division VPs, Accounting, Investments, P&C Insurance, Employee

Benefits, and Life Insurance, developed a strategy for presenting a complete financial planning practice, and how to integrate this into our client presentations.

Not to bore you, but please let me know if/when we reach that point, if one of my life insurance consultants attracted a new client, the client was told about our holistic plan to address all his/her needs, goals, and risks.

At some stage of the life insurance planning, the client's advisor would introduce the other members of the team..

You'll need to trust me here. In theory, integrated financial planning makes sense, and I would, later in my career, witness it work to varying degrees in practice. But that would not happen at The O'Connor Group.

Each division VP understood how her unit could maximize its effectiveness, but that often conflicted with other divisions. be

Others wanted to charge the client a fee for a financial plan.

The investment advisors wanted to do fee-only planning (accepting no commissions) but this conflicted with the insurance units.

Each unit had its own planning software preference, and the others claimed it could not work for them.

Problems existed about salaries, draws, bonuses, and commissions.

Each division and each consultant wanted their own support staff.

No one wanted to pay or share in the expenses of the others' divisions.

And the band played on.

When we brought these issues to O'Connor's attention, the reply remained consistent: "Work it out."

All he wanted to know was the revenue to The O'Connor Group.

Turnover became an epidemic at the VP, consultant, and staff levels.

Anyone of us could kill O'Connor back then and be celebrated. You might wonder how I lasted seven years. I built my team to succeed irrespective of the other teams. Perhaps I was selfish, but I wanted my people to prosper despite the environment.

And so we did, for a while.

Chapter 4

As I did every year-end, I reflected on my life. How did the past year work out related to my plans, goals, and vision, both from a personal and business perspective? What changes did I need to make in the new year, if any?

1991 was no different.

I may have failed to mention it, but Sean O'Connor was a brilliant guy. A financial genius, and an accountant at heart.

While the rest of us tried to put the consolidated financial planning practice together, Sean's focus remained on accounting, taxes, and computer software for both.

In 1990, he sold his EZTax Plan to Microsoft to be integrated into an Excel template. None of us knew for certain, but I heard an estimate that the sale brought him fifty million dollars.

To say that Sean O'Connor had lost interest in The O'Connor Group would be a gross understatement.

He began traveling more and bought vacation homes in Stone Harbor, New Jersey, and Sarasota, Florida.

He started buying small accounting firms, locally and regionally at first, then nationally. With its Home Office in Philadelphia, his software made this possible, serving smaller offices nationwide. In the fourth quarter of 1991, he started selling franchises of SPO Financial Services.

My life insurance sales division had grown to seven consultants and four and a half million dollars of new premiums in 1991. I had no interest in hiring additional, but I knew I would have to bring on one or two more a year to handle any attrition. My focus would be to continue growing the revenue of this core group.

My small group also attracted interest from several life insurance companies. As an independent firm, sixty percent of our Whole Life insurance sales were with Guardian Life and the other forty percent with MassMutual.

I advocated for whole life insurance, as it provided greater guarantees than universal life insurance.

We placed our term life insurance sales with several lesser-known companies; Disability Income sales to Principal and Guardian; and Annuity sales to Nationwide, Lincoln, and Allianz.

Guardian and MassMutual were of particular interest. They were top-rated mutual companies and paid dividends on their whole life insurance policies. Our advisors would receive medical benefits, E&O coverage, 401(k), and other benefits.

I had leverage, and it was time for a Come to Jesus meeting with my boss.

***

At ten o'clock, Wednesday, January fifth, I entered Sean O'Connor's impressive and expensive office. He was sitting by the fireplace with coffee, bagels, and pastries.

He stood with his hand extended. "Good morning, Frank. Happy New Year! How were your holidays?"

"Very nice, thank you, Sean. And yours?"

"Good, thanks. They seem to go so fast.

"You told Cindy you wanted to discuss your plans for the new year. That's always a great idea. What's on your mind?"

"Sean, my view from a distance is that the software development, accounting, and financial management parts of your business here are going great, and I know that may be an understatement.

Our life insurance group seems to be thriving, yet it will remain a minor component of your operations.

"In all honesty, I am unfamiliar with the other divisions, but I would speculate they are not doing so great." I paused, wanting Sean to affirm or refute.

"I would agree with your assessment."

"I need you to consider giving us a greater share of the revenue our group is producing. You're taking thirty-five percent off the top, but our rent and salary expenses are fixed and do not increase with our sales. Our guys are paying for their benefits.

"Several other insurance companies have approached them with much sweeter deals. If they leave, I cannot replace them without an enormous loss of sales. I would have to think about my future then."

"Is that a threat?"

"I did not intend it to be. I'm just trying to be honest with you, Sean. I need these advisors more than they need me and you. I need to bring them a larger piece of the pie that they are bringing us."

"If they do not need you anymore, I could eliminate you and pass along your income to them."

"As unscrupulous as that may be, you could do that, Sean."

I had expected this, and my seven reps told me, with no hesitation or qualification, that if I moved, they were coming with me, no matter what O'Connor offered them.

I added, "Since you brought that up, Sean, I also wanted to discuss my Deferred Compensation Plan. I've got close to a half million in there now."

"If I recall, Frank, you would not be 100% vested until you are here ten years."

"Correct again, but there is a provision that allows exceptions, and you could grant me 100% vesting based on my past performance and loyalty."

"So let me make certain I understand you, Lazarus. You threaten to leave and then want me to make an exception and vest your profit-sharing plan? You call that *chutzpah*, right?"

"You are on a roll, Sean."

"We both ought to give this some thought, Frank. Let's meet this time next week. Make sense?"

"Absolutely!" I stood, and we shook hands.

***

I made my decision ten minutes ago. MassMutual had already offered to cover my non-vested amount in addition to a $250,000 signing bonus, as well as bonuses for all seven of my team. They would also hire our three key staff personnel.

I called each of my team that night. MassMutual, here we come. We would take the next four days to secure our files, paper and electronic, client lists, and anything we would need to transition to MassMutual.

I sent Sean O'Connor the following email at ten o'clock on Sunday night:

Dear Sean:

This letter is to inform you of my decision to resign from The O'Connor Group, effective immediately.

I thank you for these past seven years and wish you and your family the very best in the future.

Frank Lazarus

I suggested my team send something similar at ten-thirty PM.

Chapter 5

I hope the trip down my memory lane was as good for you as it was for me. That trip reinforced my decision.

With the who and why answered, much remained to contemplate, plan, and execute.

I thought *how* I would kill O'Connor would determine *when and where*.

There are many ways to kill someone; traditional weapons, poison, fake accident, or a burglary gone bad. I could not imagine how I could poison him. It's not like he'll be inviting me to Thanksgiving dinner.

Besides, through my research, I have learned that poison is a woman's method of killing. There's no blood, no confrontation, and no physical skills needed except for getting the damn cap off the poison bottle.

But poison might also point a finger at some innocent woman, and it is my belief there could be a lengthy list of those. His wife and current mistress, for two. When you add former mistresses and employees, that list swells.

Not poison.

An accident or robbery gone bad might garner the guy sympathy. *Did you hear what happened to that poor Sean O'Connor?* The last thing I want to do is make him a martyr. No! I want everyone to know that someone hated this son-of-a-bitch so much, I murdered him in cold blood.

So that leaves me mano a mano with the weapon of choice. I'd love to use a chainsaw, but I do not own one, and I think the police would look for a recently purchased chainsaw.

Also, with my luck, I would not get the thing started. I'd be pulling that cord until I was exhausted screaming, "Don't run away Sean, I'll be right with you."

An axe? Too trite.

Knife? I'd clip his ear instead of his jugular.

Nope, it's gotta be a gun. With a silencer, since I hate loud noises.

Liberal that I am, I do not own a gun. I don't have any gun shops on my favorite website list. *Dick's* might sell them, but that's the same problem with the chainsaw.

I've got the start of an idea.

Chapter 6

In my book, *Claudia's Revenge*, Avi Golden was looking for a hitman to kill an Inquirer reporter who was nosing around some of Avi's murders. Avi recalled his buddy, the late Billy Caldwell, got involved with a gangbanger by the name of Heem Jones out in West Philly. If this Jones could hook Avi up with a gun for hire, he ought to be able to get me a gun.

Jones used Big G's Chicken Shack at Fifty-second Street as his office. I pulled into a parking spot on the street at eleven-thirty, trying to beat the lunch hour crowd, assuming there might be one.

Big G's Shack was à propos; it was a shack with four tables, a beer cooler, a counter with three stools, a grill, and a double deep-fryer. The sixty-ish, heavy-set man in a Phillies tee-shirt had the grill and both fryers working while he perused the stack of takeout orders. There is nothing quite like the aroma of cheesesteaks, fried chicken, and French fries to whet the appetite of a native Philadelphian. But I was here on business and did not want to hang around any longer than I had to.

I remembered from the book this dude's name was Cedric. "Hey Cedric, when you got a minute?"

Cedric didn't stop cooking, but looked over his shoulder. "Do I know you?"

"No, I got your name from a friend. I'm looking for Heem Jones."

With that, Cedric turned around and looked at the only other person in the place. The man was sitting alone at the table next to the beer cooler, working on his cell phone. I turned also, and said, "You Heem?" and approached his table.

"Who wants to know?"

"My name is Frank."

"Can I tell Heem what Frank might want?"

"Sure. I'm looking to buy a clean gun with a silencer. Can you help?"

"What makes you think Heem might have a gun for you?"

"I understand Heem has quite a network and can often secure such items."

"Who told you that?"

"Avi Golden ring a bell?"

"No. Should he?"

Shit! I did not use Avi's real name in the book, and I forgot to look up the alias I gave him. "How about Billy Caldwell?"

"You knew Billy? I seem to recall a white dude by the name of Walter used Avi's name a while back."

"That's it. Walter was Avi, and he and I both knew Billy."

"OK, and if Heem can help you, are you looking for something specific?"

"I heard that the Smith and Wesson M&P M2.0 has the built-in suppressor and is a reliable weapon."

"Nice, and do you have cash with you?"

"I'll get it."

"You know where George's Hill is?"

"Sure!"

"Go past the main entrance of the Mann Center to the fork in the road. Turn right and park. No one is up there during the day. I'll find you. One hour, $5,000 in cash."

"I'll be there."

I returned to my car. I looked around as if I knew what I was doing. I suspected Jones feared he was being watched at the shack here.

George's Hill (George Washington may have slept there), is in the Fairmount Park section of West Philadelphia. It's about two miles from Big G's and is best known as Lover's Lane for those without indoor facilities.

Up at George's Hill, there was no place to hide. Better for me and Jones.

I brought $10,000 in cash with me. I guess $5,000 is a good deal for an $800 gun. It's a seller's market.

We had no trouble finding each other, and Jones parked next to me. He came around to my window and handed me the package. I gave him mine with the cash.

Jones said, "You may look over the gun and the ammo while I count the cash. When I pull away, our business is concluded. Capice?"

"Capice."

We both drove off five minutes later.

Chapter 7

It was mid-May, and I wanted to be back on Hilton Head by Memorial Day. I had already determined with the research I needed to do, I would wait until my fall visit to Philly to execute the plan.

A year ago, I encountered Jamie Talarico on Facebook, and we exchanged email addresses. Jamie was a rare dude, a tech wizard in 1985, and now, at age sixty, he was still a techie. He joined O'Connor right out of the Franklin Technical Institute and, remarkably, he was still there.

Once I targeted O'Connor, I scheduled dinner with Jamie.

Jamie now lived in Broomall, a suburb in Delaware County, Delco, to its residents. Delco is not a haven for fine dining, and Jamie suggested Tavola in Springfield. A quasi-Italian/sports bar, I had eaten there several times years ago.

It was a good thing Facebook had current pictures of Jamie, as I would never have recognized him. He always had long hair and a scraggly beard, but now he was mostly bald with the scraggly beard. By reflex, we greeted each other with Bro Hugs.

"Geez, Jamie, you've aged," I said.

"No shit, Frank. I think you have also, but not as much. Good to see you; thanks for suggesting it."

Looking at a half-empty bar, I suggested we sit there. Two guys at a bar seem more natural than two guys at a table. The bartender was prompt, and Jamie ordered a Jack and Coke. I went with Tito's vodka on the rocks with a slice of orange.

"OK, thirty-four-year summary in a hundred words, go!" I demanded.

"Still a Sixers fan, same job, divorced, two kids, Jimmy and Kaitlin, ages twenty-nine and twenty-seven. Live in Broomall with Helene Rossi and her teenage daughter, Kelly. How'd I do? Your turn."

"Age seventy-eight, three kids from two ex-wives, five grandchildren, retired three years ago and became a writer. I split my time between Philly and Hilton Head. Golf game still sucks."

"Not bad. Did anything special trigger this get-together?"

Sure, I intend to kill Sean O'Connor and need some dope. "Not really Jamie. You get old, you get sentimental. I talk to John Oliver once a year, but he left O'Connor before I did. I assume Sean is retired by now; any of his kids in the business?"

"I don't think you would be shocked to hear Sean still pokes around when he is in town. Fortunately, that is less and less these days. He spends the summer down the shore and is in Swarthmore now, so he's in the office two or three days a week. He'll stay around until late December and then take his boat down to Florida for the winter.

"And yes, his son, Sean Jr. runs the business. He goes by J. R. His daughter, Kate, may be next in line. She's only a junior at St. Joe's and plays basketball there, but she has worked here the last few summers and on longer breaks. She could be the brains in the family and, unlike the male O'Connors, seems to be grounded."

"Interesting. The money still rolling in?"

"Seems to be. My focus is keeping all the affiliated offices on the network and all systems running. That's been a challenge with growth and the ever-changing tech world."

The bartender took our order for pizzas and Caesar salads, and we had second drinks.

I changed the subject, and we spent the rest of the evening discussing families, divorces, and the Philly sports teams. The Phillies were off to a good start; the Sixers fizzled again in the playoffs, and the city was holding its collective breath about Jalen Hurts and the Eagles.

I invited him to come visit me on Hilton Head, and I'd call him again on my next trip up north.

Debriefing myself on the drive home, I confirmed O'Connor still lived in Swarthmore and was back in the Philly area between September and January.

That fit into my plans perfectly.

Chapter 8

I had everything I needed, so I returned to Hilton Head the Wednesday before Memorial Day.

I have not discussed this matter with Tawana.

This was deliberate, as she would either beg me to forget this crazy idea, or she'd want to join in on the fun. Perhaps both. I did not want this to become just another date night.

Back on the Island, I got busy again with my latest novel, which I have temporarily titled, *Murder in the Lowcountry*. You can imagine how long I pondered that title. I think I need to change that. Suggestions?

You may not be familiar with the term Lowcountry. When I first got here, I thought it referred to its being at sea level, but that is incorrect.

According to Wikipedia, the term "Lowcountry" originally referred to *all of the states below the Fall Line or the Sand Hills, which run the width of the states from Aiken County to Chesterfield County. The Sandhills, or Carolina Sandhills, is a 15–60 km wide region within the Atlantic Coastal Plain province, along the inland margin* of this province. The Carolina Sandhills are interpreted as eolian (wind-blown) sand sheets and dunes that were mobilized episodically approximately 75,000 to 6,000 years ago.

    But it is easier today to think of the area from Charleston in the north to Savannah to the south, and perhaps five to fifteen miles inland.

    The weather on Hilton Head in late May is very warm, but not quite the heat and humidity of July and August. We can still go out in May, and even in June.

    Murder in the Lowcountry (MLC) is not the book you are currently reading, which is finished. MLC will be another book in the *Brown & McNeil Murder Mystery Series*. A couple of fans suggested I should write one with more appeal to my Lowcountry following, all seven of them, since my prior books were all set in the Philadelphia area.

    Today, I am off to the Palmetto Shooting Range. The indoor facility is on the plantation across the street from us. I never knew it was there. It is an isolated section, and I can hear the faint sound of gunshots as I park my car.

    I now have concerns over the element of the clientele I might encounter at a gun-shooting place in South Carolina. I'm not expecting to find any clean-shaven environmentalists in here.

Then again, there could be a few tourists from the Midwest honing their shooting skills for self-defense purposes or killing a former boss.

As I enter, the smell of gunpowder hits me. How do I know this? Have I ever smelled gunpowder before? Has the smell of the rifle range in the army's basic training stuck in my nasal subconscious?

I can see that twelve of the fifteen bays are in use. I approach the woman behind the plexiglass window and say, "Is this where I sign up?"

"Yes, sir. I gather you are not a member. Are you visiting the Island or are you a resident?"

"A resident."

"You might consider a membership. For $75 a month, you have unlimited visits. All you would pay for would be ammo and gun rental if needed. And you would be eligible for tournaments and discounts on guns and other equipment."

"Sounds like a good deal, but I think I'll pass. By the way, is this plexiglass bullet-proof?"

"No one has tested yet. Will you need to rent a gun, rifle, or ammo, sir?"

"No, I brought my own, thanks."

"Please fill this form out and bring it back to me. The cost for one hour will be twenty-five dollars."

She puts the form on the clipboard and hands it to me with a pen.

I take a seat and read through the form. Most questions seem to be identity-related. A couple of questions give me some concern:

What will you be using your weapon for? *Just to kill a former boss; is that a problem?*

Do you have a history of mental illness? *That's rather personal; do you have a need to know?*

Have you had thoughts of suicide? *Hasn't everyone?*

The name of someone in case of an emergency? *Sorry, she doesn't know I'm here.*

I turn in the form and pay my twenty-five dollars.

"Thank you, sir. Please go down to bay number seven. Harvey will meet you there and give you the orientation. Good shooting."

I see Harvey waving at me. He was certain I could not find bay seven on my own. I walk towards him.

"You must be Harvey."

"Yes sir, good guess Mr. Frank. What will you be shooting with today?"

I hand him my Smith and Wesson M&P M2.0.

"Nice," Harvey comments. "This is the one with the suppressor built-in?"

"It is. I've got thin walls and I wouldn't want to wake my neighbors when I shoot any intruder."

"That's very considerate of you, Mr. Frank. I want to review a few safety rules with you, and show you how to review your shots, and stuff like that."

He did all that in ten minutes. "You know you should never point your gun at anyone you're not intending to shoot, right?"

Assuming I know what I am doing, he sets the target at a hundred yards and leaves. I almost call him back to bring it closer to five feet, but I'll try to do it myself. I move the target to twenty-five feet. I insert the magazine, and, taking great care not to point at anyone, I aim.

I think I see the target, so I squeeze the trigger. It takes a bit more pressure, but it fires and knocks me back two feet. There was no indication I hit the target, or anyone else. I am not discouraged.

I took five more shots, hitting the margin of the target twice. I brought it to twenty feet. I also decided I like the two-handed grip, with my left hand under, and supporting my right.

By the end of the hour, I was hitting the target consistently at ten feet. I'll come back once a month to stay sharp.

Another box check-marked.

Chapter 9

Summers on Hilton Head are predictable.

Every day in July and August, you must expect 90/85, temperature and humidity. Some try to beat the heat by golfing or biking at seven in the morning when it is only 85/80.

Old people who live in apartments or condos choose to walk the air-conditioned corridors. At our place, if you decide to go to the pool, bring your own ice to cool off the water.

Despite this, it is the most popular time for tourists who bring their families to enjoy our beaches, golf courses, boating, horseback riding, dining, and shopping. The Island swells from thirty-five thousand residents to over a million people.

One cannot avoid tourists; I have tried. I have found it best to think of myself at the zoo, with the tourists being the animals. I carry peanuts and toss them to the most touristy idiots.

Summer is my least favorite time on the Island.

By mid-August, we are preparing for the hurricane season.

Before moving to the Island in 2019, I had a house in Bluffton, just off the Island. Before buying it in 2015, the realtor told me *a hurricane had not hit the Island in a hundred years*. In October 2016, Hurricane Matthews ended that hundred-year drought and knocked the crap out of Hilton Head, Bluffton, and everything within fifty miles.

I was a creature of habit and got even worse as I got older. My typical summer routine would be an early morning walk to the Shelter Cove Marina, stopping for twenty minutes and a cup of coffee at the Daily Café. Then I'd write for two to three hours, eat, take a nap, and read.

Twice a week, in the late afternoon, I'd play nine holes of golf at Bear Creek Golf Club.

That's where I was today. I teed off at 3:45 with Dave, a fellow I met there a couple of years ago. Dave also played alone late in the afternoon, so we'd often pair up.

I keep my score, but I'm not certain why. I take an occasional mulligan, concede myself the third putt, and forget my first and second attempts at getting out of the sand trap. I had a good solid forty-four today.

This might be a good time to tell you about Tawana Chaplin. I've been seeing Tawana for nine months now. Her Gullah family claims they've been on Hilton Head since 1860 but still have not shown me any evidence.

The Gullahs are West African Blacks delivered into slavery, mostly in the Carolinas and Georgia. A generous Union General granted them their freedom before the Emancipation Act, and they founded their independent territory in what is now known as the Mitchellville area on Hilton Head.

I met Tawana while she was tending bar at *All That Jazz*, a bar and eatery on the north end of the Island. She and her brother, Tyrone, also own a food truck.

I do not know her well enough yet to ask her about her light skin.

She keeps an apartment on Leg O Mutton Road, but we have keys to each other's apartment. I have suspicions that Tawana and I may not be exclusive, or, at least, she is not.

Tawana and I enjoy each other, but I don't think either of us believes *we'll live happily ever after.*

She must have some app on her phone that tells her when I'm close. When I walked in, she was standing in the kitchen with my gun resting on the counter.

"Hi dear. How was your game?"

"Not bad. A forty-four. Played with Dave."

"Look what I found?"

"Looks like my gun."

"Did I know you had a gun?"
"Sorry, you'll have to answer that one."
"I did not know you had a gun."
"See, I told you that you could answer that one."
"WTF are you doing with a gun?"
"I know you are concerned if Trump loses the election, the skinheads might come hunting the Jews and blacks.

"I thought we should have some protection. I didn't want to alarm you and hoped I would never need it."
"You think this little pea-shooter is going to battle against AK-15s?"
"It might stop the first guy through the door and scare off any others."
"You did not intend to tell me?"
"You have so much on your mind, dear, I didn't want to burden or scare you with this."
"I'm not sure I like this. Is it loaded? Do you think I need my own?"
"Yes, but the safety is on, I hope. And no, I don't even think I need it. If Trump loses, they swore they were leaving the country. I'm taking them at their word."
"Was the golf course crowded?"
For now, Tawana was satisfied.
I planned to go north in mid-October for my annual visit with friends and family. I would stay until mid-De-

cember, perhaps through Christmas. It depended on my plan to kill Sean O'Connor.

The only things I had not decided yet were when and where.

But I had the embryo of a plan. Jamie Talarico told me that O'Connor's granddaughter played for St. Joe's basketball team. The Lady Hawks' opening home game was Tuesday, December 10th. Pop-pop would be there for sure. All I would need to do is find out where he parked and wait for him after the game.

***

In late September, I visited the shooting range for what I hoped would be my last visit. Even though this was only my fifth visit, Harvey greeted me like an old friend.

"What distance do you want the target at today, Mr. Frank?"

"Twenty feet would be good, Harv. Thanks!"

"Ooh, you gonna sneak up on this rabbit, huh?"

"That's the plan."

Harvey wished me good shooting and left me to my own.

I practiced at twenty and ten feet for forty-five minutes. I hit the target consistently from these distances, with only an occasional miss. I figured I could always take a couple of shots at O'Connor if I missed the first.

Before departing, I gave Harvey a twenty-dollar tip; my usual had been five dollars.

What I still needed to do, I would do when I returned to Philly.

Chapter 10

I left Hilton Head for Philadelphia at eight a.m. on Friday, October 11th. I have made this trip many times during the twenty years I have been visiting and living on the Island.

It's a twelve-hour drive, but with my need for potty breaks, it ends up fourteen to fifteen hours. I break it into a two-day trip. I would normally stay in the Richmond area, but my daughter Laura asked me to stay with them. That's an hour and a half further, making the first day quite difficult, and the second day much easier. But I love the chance to spend time with her, Jeremy, and my grandsons, Riley and Jack.

The weather cooperates and I have a sunny, sixty-degree morning. It got cloudy as I passed South of the Border at the North Carolina state line, but as the sun faded in Virginia, it made for an orange and red sunset.

I pulled in at five-twenty and saw four eyes staring out the window, followed by the front door opening and the two boys rushing out to greet me. Laura and

Jeremy soon joined them. I packed an overnight bag besides all the other stuff I brought north, so we did not have to empty the car.

Fortunately, I remembered it was close to Halloween and brought treat baskets, Hilton Head Tee shirts, leftover beach toys, and wine for the adults.

They were keeping the pizza warm, and Jeremy made a salad. I slowed them down to make enough time for a vodka. This allowed us to discuss the drive and the boys' status, so I knew what to expect from them.

Over dinner, the boys told us about flag football, judo, soccer, and the Buffalo Bills season. When I asked about school, all I got was, "It's fine." What more could I ask?

Laura asked me about my book sales and if I was working on a new book.

"It seems, Laur, I'm always working on a new book. This will be another Brown and McNeil Mystery Murder in the Lowcountry, about a murder on Hilton Head. It just so happens when Brown and McNeil are vacationing on Hilton Head. I'm far from finished."

Once again, I did not think this was the time to discuss my book about killing Sean O'Connor.

Riley asked, "Pop-pop, how about the book you are going to write about me playing football?"

"Riley, I have not forgotten about that book, but I am finding it very difficult to write for a ten-year-old. But I'll keep trying, I promise."

I knew the kid would never forget about that.

This is an early-to-bed household, and the house was quiet by nine o'clock. This was fine for me.

Early to bed, early to rise. Jeremy at six, Laura at seven, and then the rest of us. We timed this visit to coincide with Jack's tag football game, but we woke to rain and the rain canceled the game.

We decided we would all go to Krispy Kreme, and that would make up for the missed football game.

By eleven, I was back on the road for the four-hour drive. There was no doubt I would stop at Wawa and pick up a hoagie for dinner.

I can be SO predictable.

Chapter 11

Sunday morning, I was up early, so I returned to Wawa, this time for breakfast: Sizzlies, egg, meat, and cheese sandwiches, and coffee.

A thought came to me on the ten-minute drive back. Why did I struggle with deciding whom to kill? It's three weeks before the election and campaign signs are on the lawns.

I'll feel so responsible if Harris loses this election based on Pennsylvania's vote, and a hundred votes was the difference. I could have fire-bombed fifty homes with Trump signs, and we'd all be better off.

It is, of course, not too late to change my plan, but there is no one I can discuss this with. I set up an anonymous X account and a poll asking the following question:

If you had planned to kill someone from your past who was a rotten person, but then was told that Pennsylvania would determine the Presidential election and that the margin in Pennsylvania would be one hundred votes, would you:

a) Kill the Rotten person
b) Kill 101 Trump supporters
c) a) and b)
d) Don't kill anyone

I allowed the poll to remain open for forty-eight hours and 6,500 people voted with the results:

a) 1%

b) 49%

c) 49%

d) 1%

Mr. Gallup may not sanction the results since 99% of my followers are Democrats. But I figure, why would I ask Republicans or TrumpNuts?

I hate to disappoint y'all, but I'm sticking with my original plan to kill Sean O'Connor. I know there is plenty of support for Trump in Butler, Punxsutawney, Lockhaven, and Somerset, Pennsylvania, but I am confident the American people will come through. Pennsylvania will vote for Harris, and she'll win by a comfortable margin, if not a landslide.

Back on the trail of Sean O'Connor, I needed to get a tracking device on his car. But I didn't know what kind of car he drove. I was certain it would be a very high-end, $100,000-plus car, but there were several of those on the street. Because his estate and home are gated and secure, so I couldn't sneak into his driveway.

I remembered that Claudia Campbell had a contact in *Claudia's Revenge* who got information on two vehicles owned by Avi Golden, the killer of Claudia's fiancée. What was his name? I've got the book right here.

Got it. Harvey Green. I got his phone number on Google. This would be tricky. Claudia knew Green on a personal level. I did not. And I had to use an alias in case there might be any blowback after the murder.

"Green Investigations. This is Harvey Green."

"Good morning Harvey. My name is Gabe Milstein. I'm a friend and client of Claudia Campbell. Claudia suggested I contact you."

"Claudia? I hope you're not her boyfriend. I am ga-ga for Claudia."

"Aren't we all, Harvey, but you'll get no competition from me? I can understand your attraction to her. I think she's gorgeous and intelligent and has a good soul. Her losing Melanie was just awful."

"It was for sure. How can I help you, Gabe?"

"I am looking for a car and tag number for Sean O'Connor. Claudia said you helped her with that kind of thing."

"I did, but I did it as a favor to Claudia. I'd have to charge you a thou for that. I need to pay a guy at the DMV."

"That's reasonable, Harv. How do you want to handle it?"

"Is Ardmore convenient for you?"

"Absolutely."

"Tomorrow at two o'clock, there is a bench in front of Your Average Joe's restaurant. I'll be sitting or standing by it wearing a GMU green cap. You give me the cash; I give you the info. If I have any problem getting it, I'll call you at this number. OK?"

"Perfect. See you then, and thanks, Harvey."

"No problem, Gabe."

Chapter 12

The glorious October weather continued as it was a sunny, seventy-degree, with not a cloud in the sky day. We learned it had not rained in October yet. I'm sure the farmers are complaining.

I arrived ten minutes early for my two o'clock meeting with Harvey Green. The bench in front of Joe's was vacant, but there were a couple of women standing between it and the door to the restaurant. Three younger men were standing further away, but soon left.

Five minutes later, a single man appeared from the rear lot. He was middle-aged, six-foot-two, average build. He was wearing jeans, a Phillies windbreaker, and a green baseball cap with gold lettering. I could not read it from my distance. He walked towards the bench, looked around, and sat.

It was game time. I patted the envelope inside my jacket. It felt like a thousand dollars in fifty-dollar bills. I approached the bench and Harvey looked up. The gold GMU lettering was on the cap, and underneath it, *George Mason University*.

I sat next to him and asked, "Harvey, I would guess?"

"Harvey it is, Gabe. Cash first."

I handed him the envelope, and he said, "Do I need to count it?"

"You don't need to, but I won't be offended if you do."

He took out a folded piece of paper from his pocket and handed it to me. I unfolded it and read:

SEAN O'CONNOR

Silver 2024 Maserati GranTurismo

Plate SPOCON3

I tried to figure out the vanity plate; a little hobby of mine. My SC plate is PHL2HHI. S(ean)P(middle initial)OCO (nnor) but not sure about the three. Could there be two other SPOCONs? Perhaps it was for his three kids?

I said, "Are we done here, Harvey?"

'Not so fast. A word of advice, Gabe. Never try to bullshit a private investigator. I called Claudia last night and the funny thing is, she doesn't know any Gabe Milstein."

Shit. Nailed. "Sorry, I know of Claudia, but she does not know me."

"And how would knowing Claudia get you my name?"

"A bit more complicated. I called her office and asked for the PI they used. They had a few, but the assistant thought you might be the one Claudia contacted for a personal favor. Again, sorry about that."

"OK, not a problem. Now we are finished with our business."

We stood and, not bothering with farewells, went searching for our cars.

Next, I would go to the O'Connor Group office and search the parking lot for O'Connor's car. I purchased a Lightning Model: GL300XB Tracker and Extended Battery on Amazon.

The extended battery allowed me to place the device on the car three months in advance, which was more than enough time for me, as I was now fifty-five days until K day.

Chapter 13

There was no urgency in mid-October to get the tracker device working, but I couldn't be certain when O'Connor would be in the office.

Jamie said he was in two or three days a week, but I didn't think calling him every morning to see if O'Connor was in was prudent. I thus needed to go into the city hoping his car would be in the lot, but there was no guarantee.

I figured that since his golf club was closed on Mondays, that might be a day he would go to the office.

On Monday, October twenty-first, my granddaughter's birthday, I drove to the Wynnewood train station.

The farmers were getting some rain this morning as I caught a nine-fifteen train into Philadelphia's Suburban Street Station. Suburban Station was one of the three Regional Rail Line stops in the city.

The O'Connor's World Headquarters was in Liberty Place between Sixteenth and Seventeenth Streets. Two blocks from City Hall, Liberty Place was best known for being the first building to be taller than the top of William Penn's hat on his statue atop City Hall. That was in 1986 and, once the local developers broke the gentlemen's agreement, many new, taller buildings now obscured City Hall from the Philadelphia skyline.

For followers, it was also where Avi Golden murdered Melanie Wexler in *April Fools, The Candidate*.

At five before ten o'clock, I entered the lobby of One Liberty Place and went to the elevator and the underground garage. I knew the lot was secure with CCTV cameras covering the entire four levels, and a patrolling security guard.

I purchased a dreadlock wig to wear under a Temple baseball cap and an Eagles hoodie. I was wearing my Brooks Cross-trainers and would appear to be walking for exercise. If I had to return tomorrow, I'd wear the same.

I avoided looking at the cameras and walked at a quick exercise pace. It took ten minutes to walk the four levels and, not seeing the silver Maserati, I walked back up to level one. I saw no security guard.

Shit! Just my luck; he's not here today.

I returned to the lobby, located the men's room, and removed the wig, hat, and hoodie. I replaced them with a Penn State cap and sweatshirt.

I took the escalator up to the food court and got a Pastrami and Swiss cheese on rye from Bain's Deli. No sense in wasting a trip to the city,

I caught the eleven-forty-two train back to the burbs; I'd have to repeat this process tomorrow and pray for better luck.

Chapter 14

The rain was heavier and steadier on Tuesday morning.

I'm now an hour earlier than yesterday, and I figure this is good, as I won't see anyone who saw me yesterday. When I get to Suburban Station, having time to kill, I have coffee first at Dunkin' Donuts. I suspect if Sean O'Connor is going into the office today, he might not be in at eight o'clock, choosing to wait until after the rush hour.

At nine-thirty, I walk to Liberty Place. The rain is lighter and suggests it is letting up. Like yesterday, I entered and walked right to the parking lot elevator. I got educated yesterday and discovered a section on level one for the office residents to park. Not only that, but the spots are reserved for others.

Again, being careful not to look at the cameras. I walk to that section of the lot, which is only half full.

There it is; the silver Maserati with the vanity plate.

I pause, making certain I am not in sight of the camera, and remove the tracker from my pocket. I turn it on and place it under the rear passenger side wheel cover.

I return to the lobby and check the app on my iPhone. The red light is blinking, showing the car. I'm back in the men's room and discard the wig in the trash can.

Since it is too early for lunch, I go to a different Dunkin', have a second cup of coffee, and reward myself with a Boston Creme donut. This undercover work is taxing, and I deserve it.

I get the outbound train back to Wynnewood at ten-twenty and go to my old office. I still do this every time I am up north, even though there are always fewer people who remember me.

It's now closer to lunchtime. My first thought was Hymie's, but I had a pastrami yesterday. That, and it was more likely I'd run into old neighbors or friends.

I have a flash of brilliance and head to Larry's on Fifty-fourth Street on the St. Joe's campus. Larry's is one of a hundred iconic cheesesteak shops in Philly, and the *Home of the Bellyfiller.*

Larry's has changed little since its move from the Overbrook High School campus three miles away. The lunch crowd was an eclectic group of college students, blue-collar workers, business people, and neighborhood blacks. I was the only old white guy in the place.

I opted for a cheesesteak, cheese wiz, and fried onions. I add ketchup and chase it with a Diet Coke. This would ruin dinner and any chance of having a decent night's sleep.

Between bites, I again checked on the tracker, and it was still flashing in the same location.

I then get in my car and circle the St Joe's campus. The original Hawk Hill campus started at City Avenue and Fifty-fourth Street, went down to Overbrook Avenue, then to Wynnefield Avenue to Cardinal Avenue, and back to City Avenue. It is about six square blocks.

The campus has expanded over the years to the suburban side of City Avenue, as well as north, south, and east of the original campus. The Hagan Arena parking lot entrance was right across the street from Larry's and would be the likely spot for O'Connor to park. That would be problematic if O'Connor stayed until the end of the game and came out with the crowd.

But I never parked on that lot as that only entrance was also the only exit, and four thousand cars exiting at the same time challenged my patience. There was a good amount of street parking on those side streets, and Cardinal Avenue was my preference.

I was counting on one of two things; if O'Connor did park on the lot, he'd leave early to beat the crowd or he'd park on the street as I would.

We would soon see.

Chapter 15

With the planning finished, the waiting began.

November in Philadelphia was much like March in reverse. In like a lamb, out like a lion. You might golf through mid-November and be shoveling snow on Thanksgiving. At least before global warming kicked in. And it seemed the coldest day would be the Saturday of the Army-Navy game.

I spent much of November dining and visiting with friends. This gave me a chance to visit my favorite dining spots in the western suburbs; *Hymie's Deli, Aldar Bistro, Pescatore, and Pepperoncini.*

One day, I took the train into town, met my daughter, Lindsay, and visited the Reading Terminal Market for a roast pork sandwich at *DiNici's*. Another day, I went to New Jersey for brunch with the Watsons, and then to Pitman to see my granddaughter play tennis.

November is also a huge month for sports in Philadelphia. By Thanksgiving, we would know about the Eagles, and this year, it appeared a .500 season was their destiny.

The Sixers and Flyers seasons were just starting, and without reading the paper or ESPN.com, you could guess the Sixers would make the playoffs and soon evaporate, and the Flyers would add to their fifty years of mediocrity, or worse.

For the last six years, I have been very fortunate, as my daughter-in-law, Michelle, has hosted Thanksgiving. My daughter Laura's family comes up from Virginia, and Dr. Lindsay has been available, making it an even dozen of us. The day starts early, and I am on my way to Pitman, New Jersey, at nine o'clock to watch the three boys play flag football.

After picking up coffee at Wawa, I arrive at ten-twenty. It is an overcast, chilly fifty degrees and I know I won't be able to spend more than an hour here. I spot my granddaughters waving at me and I walk towards them. I see my son officiating one of the games, and two of my three grandsons.

There's a time-out on the field and Riley comes running up to me. "Did you see my touchdown, pop-pop?"

"I'm sorry, Riley, I just got here. You'll have to score another one so I can see it. Did Noah score one?"

"I don't know. Not against my team." He's off.

Four teams are playing a round-robin. It's fun to watch seven to ten-year-olds in Eagles Jerseys, except for my two who are in Chiefs and Bills jerseys. They emulate the mannerisms of the players they have seen on TV and appear to be much cockier than they are.

I join the family on the sidelines, and I beg Halle and Felicity to hug me to keep me warm. That six-second hug did wonders for me.

While Riley's and Noah's teams play for the championship, my youngest grandson, Jack, and I have a catch on the sideline. With one eye on the ball and the other on the game, I see Noah catch a touchdown pass, slam the ball to the turf, and do a celebratory dance.

But Riley's team rallies for the win, the championship, and it's their turn to dance.

We return to the house, and my daughter Lindsay is there with Michelle.

We have time for another cup of coffee while Jeremy is carving the turkey. We eat early as Laura's family wants to be on the road to Virginia by two o'clock.

Age has its rewards as I get a seat at the head of the table and my own turkey leg.

Like many families, we go around the table telling what we are thankful for. I'm certain if we played last year's tape, we would see little deviation. That does not diminish the emotion for me when I tell them I am thankful for them, our health, and once again, all being together.

Larry's family is considering moving to Maryland, so this could be our last Thanksgiving in Pitman.

Laura's family loads up their car and departs at two o'clock, as they promised. Lindsay and I follow soon thereafter.

I am thankful for one more Thanksgiving with my family. This time next year, I'll either be in jail, dead, or a hunted murderer.

Chapter 16

Tuesday, December 10th, was like any other early December day in Philadelphia, except that it was the day I would become a murderer. I'm not certain anyone else in Philly could say that. Or at least not many people could say that.

But I still had time to change my mind.

I pretended to go about my morning routine of Wordle, Connections, coffee and bagel, and writing. My mind, though, is preoccupied with tonight. I always considered myself a good guy. I would give my bus seat to a pregnant woman (if I ever took a bus), hold the doors for men and women, allow grocery shoppers with one or two items to go in front of me at the checkout, and only cheat a bit on my taxes.

Now I want to be a first-degree murderer?

Yes!

I'm seventy-eight years old and people say I should take chances, get out of my routine, shake it up a bit. If I don't do it now, when will I do it?

And, at my age, what is a lifetime in jail? Perhaps two or three years? Besides, look at all the work I've done; bought a gun and learned how to shoot it, placed the tracker on Sean O'Connor's car, and bought Jamie Talarico dinner. And last night, I moved the gun to my glove compartment in the car.

Yep, I'm staying the course.

The game starts at seven o'clock, and at six, O'Connor's car was on the move, heading towards the St. Joe's campus. I only live fifteen minutes from campus, but I needed a parking spot of my own, so I left at six-thirty.

I always parked strategically at St. Joe's on the South side of Cardinal Avenue, just off City Avenue. This allowed easy access to City Avenue and a fast getaway. I even did this on nights when I was not committing a murder.

When I arrived at six-forty-five, two cars had beat me to that spot, but being the third car would be fine. I parked and shut off the engine. I walked to a nearby Wendy's and ordered a burger, fries, and coffee. I took my laptop so I could do some writing while killing time.

O'Connor's car was a mile from campus, so I watched it as it went to Cardinal Avenue and parked ten cars behind me, also facing City Avenue. I told you O'Connor was sharp.

The only way for me to follow the game was on St. Joe's network. Not exactly ESPN, but it would serve its purpose.

A couple of final thoughts. Since I was unaware of when O'Connor might leave the game, I had to wait near his car. And I still did not know if he would be alone.

More problematic, I knew there were CCTV cameras at the intersection of City and Cardinal Avenues. Would the police trace every car that went through that intersection around the time of O'Connor's death? I guessed there would be fifty to one hundred cars or more. I had to assume they would check us all out.

But I would tell them I was at the game and left early. I doubted they would know I worked for O'Connor thirty years ago. Knowing the neighborhood, the police would think it was just as likely the perp escaped on foot.

Was I overthinking things? Probably, but murderers did that.

With ten minutes remaining in the game, Iona was leading St. Joe's by fifteen points. If I were at the game, I'd be thinking about leaving. I assumed O'Connor might think the same.

I packed up and returned to my car, leaving the laptop and retrieving the gun. I put on gloves and put my hoodie up. I walked down Cardinal Avenue and saw the Maserati. I walked fifty feet past it and took a seat on the stone wall next to the sidewalk.

Two minutes later, as I stared at my iPhone, I saw two people walking towards me. Shit. But as they got closer and walked under the streetlight, I could see it was not Sean O'Connor but another man, presumably with his teenage daughter. They walked by me and went to the first car. First to arrive, first to leave.

Five minutes later, a single man is walking towards me. He is walking with a slight limp and hunched up in respect of the cold. When he walks under the streetlight, I can see it is Sean O'Connor.

I bound off the wall and waited for him to come to me. He intends to walk by me, avoiding eye contact. But I step in front of him.

"You're not going to say hello, Sean?"

He's startled but stops. He looks into my eyes, searching for some recognition. Finally, it registers.

"Frank? Frank Lazarus? What the hell are you doing here?"

"Waiting for you, of course. Did your granddaughter play tonight?"

"Briefly, at the end of the first half. Made the only shot she took. What is it you want, Frank?"

"Nothing, Sean. I just came to kill you." I reveal my gun.

"What the hell. Are you serious?"

"Don't I look serious?"

"Why, what; put that away."

"I don't have time to chat, Sean. This is for all your past sins."

Before he could say another word, I put two bullets into his chest. He drops to the ground with blood oozing out. I removed his watch and wallet to make it appear a robbery. I retrieved the tracker from his car.

I see no one else approaching, and no cars drive past me. But I know someone will discover him within the next ten minutes. I walk to my car and drive off, turning right on City Avenue.

I stop at a 7-11 dumpster and toss my gloves and hoodie, but then realize one more potential problem. I was going to toss the gun into the Schuylkill River on the way home, but I remembered Tawana knows I have the gun, presumably to protect us from skinheads.

I needed to think about this, so I put the gun back in the glove compartment.

I'll be home ten minutes later.

Chapter 17

I had a restless night's sleep.

There was some exhilaration of having pulled it off and completed my mission. But I'm not a psychopath, and I felt the burden of having taken a life. I hoped in time, I would come to grips with this dichotomy.

Right now, I would have preferred to be on Hilton Head. I planned to return on Saturday, the twenty-first, still ten days away.

The next morning I turned on the local news, something I had not done in fifteen years. O'Connor's murder was the lead story, but there were few details, including the identity of the deceased.

I then checked the online version of the Inquirer, but the article had nothing more and still had not identified O'Connor. I knew this would become a high-profile investigation since O'Connor was a well-known business and community leader.

I had to assume at some point, they would contact everyone that CCTV captured license plates. What would they think when they saw my South Carolina license plate?

I no longer had a Pennsylvania address, so I did not think they would knock at my door anytime soon. They could get my address on Hilton Head, but will they come down to interview me? I wouldn't think so unless they had found something else, and I was certain they would not.

Four or five high school friends are good enough to be available on my once-a-year visit to the Philly area. It's a chance to catch up, find out who has died or is getting ready to, and see who can remember what from those *good old days.*

When I step out the door, I am reminded why I need to get back down south; forty friggin degrees feels like ten to my newly infused Southern blood. And it's blustery, and whatever leaves are still around from the fall clean-up are being recirculated.

I always forget that I can start the car from the warm comfort of my living room, but alas, I sit there for a minute or two, waiting for the heat to kick-in.

At nine o'clock, there is still plenty of metered parking along Montgomery Avenue. I park six spots from Hymie's front door and see Nate and Lee entering. I feed the meter, perhaps the last one in America that still accepts quarters. As I enter, I see Coop is there also and the three have just sat down at a booth set for six.

"There he is, the man of the hour," Lee exclaims. I look over my shoulder towards the front door to see whom he might be referring. I see no one and proceed to the table.

"I know you're not talking about me. You expecting Billy?"

"No, but Jay should be here."

They stood, and we all hugged.

"Why not look at menus first?" I suggested, knowing that everyone had long ago memorized the menu and knew what they were having.

"When are you going back to Hilton Head?" Nate asks.

"About ten days, if I can stand the cold for that long. Does forty degrees feel colder as we get older?"

"It's all about the wind chill," Coop brilliantly contributes.

As the waitress is filling our coffee cups, Jay enters and the four of us get up to repeat the hugging routine.

We get settled and start with medical updates. A couple of the guys see my former cardiologist, but the good news is this group of seventy-eight-year-olds are all doing quite well, thank you.

We place our orders and when the server leaves, Lee asks, "Did you hear about the murder at St. Joe's last night?"

Hymie's is about two miles from the St. Joe's campus and Lee and Jay grew up in that neighborhood.

I say, "I saw it on the news this morning, but no details. What happened?"

"The guy had been to the Fieldhouse for a basketball game and someone shot and robbed him on Cardinal Avenue. No one saw anything, of course. But they hope to have CCTV."

"That neighborhood has gone to shit. It was a great place to grow up, but now, I don't even go to Larry's for a Bellyfiller."

"Overbrook Park isn't any better, I'm afraid," Nate adds.

"There's no chance they'll catch the killer. Does killing someone for twenty bucks make sense?"

"A rhetorical question, right?"

I was feeling uncomfortable by the conversation, and relieved when it switched to the Eagles, who were eight and six with three games remaining.

The server interrupted to deliver an assortment of smoked salmon, omelets, French Toast, bacon, and scrapple. She waited while we all perused each other's plates to make certain we had the right order, and nothing was missing. After requests for more coffee, butter, and napkins, we dismissed her.

We spent the next hour with more of the same. It was the same discussion we had last year this time. That's the great part of being quasi-senile. We settled the bill and walked out together. More man hugs and fond farewells.

God Willing, same time next year.

Chapter 18

The next morning, I went to Wawa and got coffee, a breakfast sandwich, and the Inquirer. I rarely buy a newspaper anymore but the newsfeeds I get online only cover world and national news. I was quite certain the online edition of The Island Packet would not cover a Philadelphia murder story unless they knew the murderer was a Hilton Head resident.

The two-day-old story still made it to the front page, but now appeared *below the fold.*

NO SUSPECTS IN THE O'CONNOR MURDER

Two days after the murder of Philadelphia businessman, Sean O'Connor, the Philadelphia police still have no suspects.

Someone murdered O'Connor Tuesday night between nine and nine-thirty in an apparent robbery on Cardinal Avenue on the Saint Joseph's University campus.

The Delaware County resident had left a Lady Hawks basketball game where his granddaughter played for the Hawks.

No one has come forward as a witness to the crime.

West Philadelphia's senior detective Vernon Brown was assigned the case and told the media, "While we do not have any suspects yet, we have the license plates from seventy-five cars that went north or south on Cardinal Avenue in the time frame. We will contact all seventy-five car owners. But it is just as likely that the killer was on foot and disappeared into the neighborhood. We need the help of the residents who may have seen anything.

"We have learned the weapon used was a Smith and Wesson M&P M2.0 with a built-in suppressor. We are checking gun registrations and local gun shops for recent purchases."

Detective Vernon Brown? I created Detective Vernon Brown in my first book, *THE MURDER GAMBIT*. How can this be? This is spooky shit.

I knew they would identify the gun, but it's not registered. Would the police contact Heem Jones? They most likely know Jones is a gangbanger and could deal in weapons. But if Heem admitted selling the gun, he would implicate himself in the murder. And he did not know my real name.

Perhaps I should buy another gun and toss this one in the river. Tawana would not notice the difference. But I couldn't go back to Jones, and I don't know any other street gun dealers.

A better idea comes to mind. When I return to Hilton Head, I can visit my old buddy, Harv at the gun range.

I'm sure he'll have an old one he can sell me. Then I'll throw this gun into the Broad Creek instead of the Schuylkill River.

I need to chill until I can get out of Dodge next week.

Meanwhile, I continued to think about Detective Vernon Brown.

Chapter 19

The next week added nothing much to the story. No suspects or witnesses, even though the police said they were still calling all the drivers caught on CCTV.

The Philadelphia Business Journal ran a story on The O'Connor Group and the death and legacy of its Founder, Sean O'Connor. Employees, clients, and family were all quoted, and believed this to be a random act of violence.

There were more calls for greater security on the St. Joseph's campus and tougher gun laws.

There is no mention of any disgruntled former employees.

I spoke with Tawana last night; she was eager to know when I'd be home. I was more than ready to head south and made one more visit to Pitman to see my son's family and had dinner with my daughter Lindsay.

On Saturday, the 21st, I took off at six AM. I would decide by four o'clock how tired I was and whether

I could make it to Hilton Head or needed to stop in northern South Carolina for the night.

It was cold but dry and that's all I could hope for. It would get warmer as the afternoon came, and I got further south. I made great time through Philly, Delaware, and Maryland. Then I experienced the expected slowdown as I hit the DC area, but an hour later, I was back on track.

I wanted to see if I could make it to the Island in one day, something I had not done now in fifteen years. But I would not forsake the demanded bathroom, leg-stretching, and coffee breaks.

At three o'clock, I reached the Smithfield Outlet Mall in North Carolina and knew I could not get to the Island. Using my Hilton App, I reserved a room at the Hampton Inn in Florence, South Carolina, just two hours away. That would leave me with an easy three-hour drive on Sunday.

While I did not know it, it also gave me a much-needed alibi for another crime.

Chapter 20

Friday morning the 20th, Detective Vernon Brown arrived at the Dunkin Donuts at Fifty-Second and Chestnut Streets at seven-twenty. Once a week, maybe twice, he would meet his buddy James McNeil.

I had created both men in *THE MURDER GAMBIT*, when Captain Webster assigned Brown to investigate the hit-and-run murder of James's father right outside this Dunkin. The two learned they had much in common, including attending nearby West Philadelphia High School. They became good friends, and they socialized with and without their spouses.

More recently, Brown investigated the murder of Avi Golden, a sexual serial killer who murdered Melanie Wexler. Wexler was James McNeil's granddaughter's romantic partner. The story became the basis for *CLAUDIA'S REVENGE*.

Then I found out that McNeil and Brown are real people. Perhaps I somehow knew of them and used them subliminally in my books? I am hoping you can help me with this.

James McNeil arrived at seven-thirty and nodded to Brown as he got in line to order his coffee and a Boston Creme donut. Vernon stood to greet him with a bro-hug.

"Been here long, bruh?" McNeil asked.

"Nah, maybe ten minutes. What's going on, James?"

"Not much Vern. Did you catch the St. Joe murderer yet?"

"Not yet, and no solid leads. No witnesses, of course. There were only five thousand people at the game and a hundred cars parked on Cardinal Avenue. But no one saw nothing."

"You know, my friend, this could hurt Larry's business. Anything develop out of the license plates you pulled off CCTV?"

"Not yet. We are through half of them, but five are out-of-sate; two Jersey, two Delaware, and one South Carolina. Of the forty we spoke to, fifteen were at the game and the rest were coming from school or some other benign drive-through. Other than did they see anything, what more can we ask them? We could have spoken with the murderer and never knew it."

"My money is on a neighborhood kid. Only about a thousand un-registered guns in that one square mile area."

"I fear you may be right. But since this was a well-known business owner rather than a gangbanger, the case will remain open for another month or two. Changing the subject, I see Nova and Bo are off to a great start. Will this be his last season at Nova?"

Bo Campbell is James McNeil's grandson, and a highly recruited basketball star from Overbrook High School in West Philadelphia. After being recruited by the national powerhouse programs, he stayed close to home and attended Villanova University.

In his senior year in high school, the Philadelphia police charged him with murdering his best friend, and the story behind THE PHENOM was born.

"Bo promised his parents he would get a degree, so the current thinking seems to be that he will play one more year at Nova and then get his remaining credits in the offseason. It might depend on his draft projection. But this is all rather fluid, as you might imagine, Vern."

"I'll bet. Don't forget tickets for the St. Joe's game in January at the Palestra. You owe me."

"Why is it every time you ask for something, you add, *You owe me?* And I did not forget tickets for you."

"Because you do owe me, or did you forget?"

"How could I forget? You remind me every time we're together. Why not ask me for one huge favor and be done with it?"

Vernon Brown had suspected that Claudia Campbell, James's granddaughter, had killed Avi Golden, but given the lack of evidence and the relief that Golden was out of the way, no one seemed to care who killed him. Sort of a Jack Ruby thing.

"Fair enough. I'll work on that," Brown said. "I gotta run, stay in touch, and out of trouble."

"Always my brother."

Brown took off, and McNeil refilled his coffee. He had nowhere else to go for another hour.

Chapter 21

I was back on the Island at eleven-fifteen, and after stopping for a car wash and Kroger's for necessities, I was back in my apartment at noon.

It was that time of the year on Hilton Head when you needed heat until ten AM, nothing until about one, and then air conditioning until seven PM; then repeat. The apartment was a bit cool, but I left the heat off.

I opened the patio and put the cushions back on the furniture. I re-plugged the appliances. I turned the oven and microwave clocks back one hour.

I unpacked and decided to go for a walk before the one o'clock Eagles game. I wasn't certain the Eagles game would be on local TV as the NFL considers the Panthers, Falcons, and Jacksonville, home teams for us and thus would pre-empt any other Fox broadcasts.

I texted Tawana of my arrival and invited her for my default Sunday night football dinner of wings and pizza.

It was twelve-thirty before I left for my one-hour walk down to the Shelter Cove Marina and back. Christmas and New Year's weeks were always busy on the Island, interrupting the usual quiet winters we enjoyed from November through February.

The marina was busy, and many owners decorated their boats for the holiday season. I could not imagine putting an inflated Santa on the top of my boat, but hey, that's me.

I skipped my usual coffee stop at the Daily Cafe and got back to my apartment at one-forty. I quickly showered and sat down in front of the TV to learn I was being blessed with the Giants-Falcons game. Atlanta was leading 20-3, with two minutes remaining in the half.

The Eagles were leading Washington at half-time by 17-10. I muted the TV, followed the Eagles game on the ticker, and caught up on email, Wordle, and Connections.

At three-thirty, with the Eagles win assured, I could relax. Tawana still had not returned my text message, so I called her and got her voicemail. "Hello, it's me, as in Frank. It won't change my order too much, but I might add pepperoni if you're not joining me. Let me know."

I am SO predictable. At four o'clock, I make myself a double vodka on the rocks and nuke a bag of popcorn.

The four-thirty game was Jaguars vs. Raiders; I had as much interest in that as I had in who might be the next Pope.

At four-thirty, I called in my order to Giuseppe's, adding pepperoni to only half, still hoping I'd hear from Tawana.

The Sunday night game was Tampa Bay at Dallas. Dallas is the only team in the league that plays seventeen home games. I won't turn on that game unless Dallas is losing big and I'll tune in to see Jerry Jones's face of despair.

At nine o'clock, I go to bed, watch an episode of *Dexter,* and then turn in, still with no message from Tawana.

Chapter 22

I'm up at seven and go through my usual morning routine of stretching, Wordle and Connections, reading my email and news summaries, making coffee, and moving to my office to write.

At ten o'clock, I make a second cup of coffee and a toasted bagel. Twenty minutes later, I think I hear my doorbell ring. I say, *think* because with my hearing aids out, I'm never quite certain. But then there is a second banging, and someone is definitely at my door.

I peek through the peephole, and sure enough, a white guy and a black woman are staring at my eyeball. *How did they get into the building,* I wonder?

I open the door, confused. "Hello?"

"Good morning. Mr. Lazarus?" the male asks.

"Yeah?"

"I am Beaufort County Detective Hampton, and this is my partner, Detective Pickney. May we come in, please?"

Oh shit, I think. *Did the Philly police send these two to ask about my car outside St. Joe's the night of the O'Connor murder?*

"Sure, officers, please come in. Did someone admit you into the building?"

"We stopped in the office first."

I led them into my living room. "Please have a seat. What's up?"

Detective Hampton continued, "May I ask where you were this past Friday and Saturday?"

This is not about the O'Connor murder.

'Well, sure. Friday I was in Philadelphia packing and preparing to return to Hilton Head. Saturday, I was on I-95 from seven AM until about five PM, then I spent the night at a Hampton Inn in Florence. I completed the drive here on Sunday morning."

"Can anyone confirm this?"

"I was alone, but I'm sure there were some tolls on I-95; you can check my EZ-Pass account. I can find my receipt from the Hampton Inn."

I grabbed my iPhone and retrieved the email receipt from yesterday. I handed my phone to Detective Pickney, who was sitting closer.

"May I ask again what this is about, detectives?"

Ignoring my questions, "Can you tell us about your relationship with Tawana Chaplin?"

"This is about Tawana? Has something happened to her?"

"Yes, someone murdered her in her apartment on Saturday morning. Now, about your relationship?"

"Tawana murdered? That can't be true."

I cannot speak. I am bewildered, confused, and saddened in one fell swoop. I sit in silence, pondering what I have just heard. It makes no sense at all to me.

Then I recall I have a murder weapon in my house somewhere. I hope I did not leave it on the bed. *They cannot search the place, can they? I mean, probable cause, warrants, and all that shit?*

"I'm sorry, detectives. This is a shock. Can you tell me anything about what happened? I tried to reach her several times yesterday. I was hoping she would join me here for pizza and football."

"Tell us about your relationship."

"We've been seeing each other for nine months. I was alone at the bar of *All That Jazz*, where she tended bar on the weekends. The music had not started yet, and the place was not very crowded.

"We got to talking; I learned she was single. I thought she was very attractive, and I was not the first to hit on her at the bar. I asked her out, and we hit it off. That's the story."

"Did it concern you she was black?" I noticed the shocked look Detective Pickney gave her partner.

"Really, detective? 2024 on Hilton Head? No, the thought never entered my mind. I know I'm in South Carolina, but I usually only think about that when I see a Confederate Flag on the back of an F-150."

"Any disagreements, arguments, fights?"

"Only when the Falcons play the Eagles. Or what to watch next on Netflix?"

"Tawana's mother thinks you killed her daughter."

"Of course she does. The eighty-two-year-old black woman learns her fifty-three-year-old daughter is dating a seventy-eight-year-old white guy. I can understand how she feels.

"Detectives, I know you must do whatever you need to check me out, but you should be out looking for someone who may have killed Tawana, rather than wasting your time investigating me.

"There are two things that might help, but these are just suspicions, not facts. First, I think Tawana dated other men. Since she tended bar at *All That Jazz*, we never dated on weekends and often she would cancel plans at the last minute during the week. I never confronted her, but I never stopped using condoms, either.

"The other is, I'm not certain her brother is a good guy. I'm not suggesting he killed her, but I think something is going on with him other than driving the food truck. Any other questions?"

They stood, and Hampton said, "I think we are good for now, Mr. Lazarus. Thank you for your time. Do you have any plans to return to Philadelphia anytime soon?"

"Only if the Eagles win the Super Bowl. I missed the parade last time. Otherwise, I'm here until after Labor Day."

"We'll be in touch. Thank you again."

Do you appreciate the irony? I am an unsuspected murderer in Philadelphia and an innocent murder suspect on Hilton Head.

Where is that friggin gun?

Chapter 23

Tawana's mother deferred the funeral until after Christmas, not that anyone who knew Tawana would have a merry one.

I wanted to pay my respects before the funeral, so on the 26th, I went to the large trailer home of Millie Chaplin in the Spanish Wells neighborhood on the north end of the Island.

Mobile homes were prevalent in many of the original Gullah neighborhoods, even though they had been there for eighty years or more. I remember being told that since they did not have deeds to the property, they could not build permanent structures, but mobile homes skirted this law.

I had only been here once before. Tawana told me about her mom's concerns, and that it would be best to give her time. We never got that time.

Before I could knock at the door, Tawana's daughter, Anyika, stepped out onto the stoop. She threw her arms around me silently, and I whispered, "I'm so sorry," into her ear. We held on to each other. I felt her tears on my cheek, or *were they mine*?

Anyika was Tawana's twenty-three-year-old daughter. After getting her graphic design degree from SCAD two years ago, she moved to Atlanta and shared an apartment there. She worked at Coca-Cola Headquarters.

I had been with her only twice, but we made a good connection.

"How's your Grammy doing?"

"No worse than any of us, Frank. How are you doing with this?"

"About the same, Annie. I guess you know I'm a suspect, even though I was in Philly and my car during the time in question. The cops should be able to verify that. I want you to know, Annie, I had nothing to do with this and am saddened by your mom's death."

"I know that, Frank, but my Grammy needs someone to blame, and for now, that's gotta be you. I'm not certain it's a good idea for you to come into the house. I'll tell my mom you were here."

"How about the funeral tomorrow?"

"Same, but I'll be here until January 3rd, and I hope to see you. I want to discuss something or someone with you."

"I'll be around, Annie, and would love to talk to you. Call or text me when it is best for you. I got nothing going on."

"I'll do it, Frank, and thanks for stopping by. See you soon."

Chapter 24

Annie contacted me the day after the funeral, and we made plans for her to dine at my place the next night, Saturday. We agreed that would be better than whispering in a crowded restaurant, and we could watch football. The NFL did not play on Saturday, but there were several college bowl games.

She said she would bring dessert, and since I couldn't find Bassets Ice Cream on Hilton Head, I approved.

Annie arrived at five-thirty, and I buzzed her up. We hugged, and I threw her coat on the bed in the spare bedroom.

Annie was one of those gorgeous young women who seemed oblivious to her good looks. I'm certain the guys in Atlanta gave her plenty of attention, but she remained grounded. I had to remind myself that I dated her mother and had two daughters older than her.

"What are you drinking these days, Annie?"

"What do you have?"

"You know my bar is well-stocked; test me."

"Got any Prosecco?"

"Oh, don't tell me, you want an Aperol Spritz? Where was this drink five years ago? Who decides to make a drink trendy? And, YES, I of course have Prosecco and Aperol. Coming right up."

"Calm down, Frank. You asked. I would have been happy with Pinot Grigio."

"My pleasure Annie. You know, it was your mom who introduced me to Aperol."

I made two. Since I was opening the Prosecco, I thought I might as well join her. I delivered the drinks and a plate of garlic parmesan chicken wings, celery, and blue cheese dressing to the coffee table. I even remembered the extra bowl for the wing bones.

"Wow, Frank. You have been hard at work. Is that chili I smell? All this for me? You shouldn't have."

"I do this every Sunday, Annie. Your mom never told you? Speaking of, here's to your mom," raising my glass in a toast.

"To my mom," we clinked glasses.

"Let's talk, Annie. What's on your mind?"

"I don't know, Frank. I can't imagine who wanted to kill my mom. But, I've always thought my Uncle Ty was a bit of a sleazeball. I can't imagine he would kill his sister, but listen to this. Two months ago, my mom told me he and my father were scheming over the phone. She did not hear any details, but they divorced for ten years, and the son-of-a-bitch never gave my mom a dime. And he and my uncle are in cahoots on something? It makes no sense to me."

"Did you mention this to the police, Annie? I don't even know your father's name."

"I did not. I wanted to talk to you first. You think I should? My dad's name is Anton Mitchell."

"Funny, I also mentioned your uncle to the police. Let me think about this and I'll let you know. I think it could be relevant. You know, the mystery writer in me is going to do some investigating on my own. We'll talk before you go back to Atlanta next week.

"Annie, did your mom share anything else about her private life with you? Other men, perhaps? Anything about work? Your mom and I cared for each other, but I somehow sensed she was holding something back."

"Geez, I don't think so; now you've got me wondering. If I think of anything, I'll let you know."

I appreciate your sharing this with me, Annie. Another drink?"

"You're not planning to take advantage of me, are you? Sure. It's a short drive, and you have that extra bedroom if needed."

If she only knew!

We enjoyed the chili, cornbread, and buffalo coleslaw. Annie's bourbon chocolate-laced pecan pie was perfect. We emptied the bottle of Prosecco.

And Annie drove home and texted me upon her arrival.

Chapter 25

New Year's Eve fell on a Tuesday this year.

I was never a huge NYE fan. I recall my dad saying it was amateur night; all the young people who've never been out think it's a license to go crazy. The roads are like a Demolition Derby.

I planned to be All That Jazz with Tawana, but now I thought I would have an early dinner at Dockside on Skull Creek. Then I could join some friends at the WaterWalk in the Hospitality Room at eight o'clock.

They say nine is the new midnight, and I was hoping I could make it until nine o'clock.

It was a chilly forty-two degrees at eight AM, so I wrote until eleven when I expected the temperatures to be around sixty-five.

I walked my usual route and stopped for coffee at the Daily Cafe. I checked my email and saw I had a phone message. I programmed my phone not to ring unless the caller is in my Contacts. Nothing I hate worse than talking to strangers, even though talking to friends is a close second. I don't need to listen to the message; I can read it:

  HELLO MR. LAZARUS. THIS IS VERONICA AT THE PHILADELPHIA POLICE DEPARTMENT. PLEASE RETURN THIS CALL AS SOON AS YOU RECEIVE THIS MESSAGE. THANK YOU.

  I knew this day would come, but on New Year's Eve?

  Oh well, Veronica doesn't know when I got her message. Let her stew for a while.

  When I got home, I showered and had a bite to eat. I opened the NOTES app on my phone and reviewed again my cheat sheet for this call:

  YES, I PARKED ON CARDINAL AVENUE THAT NIGHT
  I WENT TO THE LADY HAWKS BASKETBALL GAME
  I STAYED UNTIL THE END OF THE GAME, BETWEEN NINE AND NINE-THIRTY
  ABOUT A TEN-MINUTE WALK TO MY CAR
  I PARKED ON CARDINAL AVENUE AND TURNED RIGHT ONTO CITY AVENUE
  I SAW NOTHING, SORRY OFFICER

  I hit the call button on my phone.

  "Philadelphia Police Department, this is Veronica."

  "Veronica, my name is Frank Lazarus, and I am returning your call."

  "Give me a sec, please. Oh yes, thank you for returning my call. Do you know why I am calling Mr. Lazarus?"

"I'm not sure; are you selling raffle tickets for the Police & Fire Benevolent Fund?"

"No sir, I am calling about a murder several weeks ago. We have a picture of your car on Cardinal Avenue at the approximate time of the murder. Do you recall that night?"

"I do, officer. I was at the basketball game at the Fieldhouse, and the next morning at breakfast a couple of friends who grew up near there mentioned it."

"When did you leave the game?"

"I stayed until the bitter end."

"Do you often go to basketball games at St. Joe's?"

"Not often, but I'm a St. Joe's Alum and I try to get to a few games when I am up in Philly. With all the hype about Caitlin Clark, I thought I'd try a women's game. I saw the men play the prior week."

"Who won the game?"

"Iona. I don't recall the final score, but think it was by about fifteen points."

"And then what?"

"And then I walked to my car and the right turn on City Avenue. I was home in fifteen minutes."

"Where's your home, Mr. Lazarus? We could not find an address other than in Hilton Head."

"When I am up in Philly, I stay at a friend's in Oak Hill Condos in Penn Valley."

"Did you see anything at all on Cardinal Avenue?"

"By the time I got to my car, half the cars were gone, and others were getting in their cars like me. But I saw nothing unusual."

"Are you sure? Any little thing?"

"Like what? I wasn't looking for anything. I focused on my driving. Sorry, but other than people getting into their cars, I saw nothing unusual."

"That's enough for now, Mr. Lazarus. We'll be in touch if we have any further questions. Thank you for your time."

"That's OK, good luck finding your murderer."

That went according to script, but I doubted that would be the end.

Chapter 26

With the holidays over, I wanted to look at this Anton Mitchell and Tyrone Chaplin unlikely alliance. If anything was going on, Mitchell had to be the brains, as Tyrone had a limited supply.

And I thought a good place to start would be with my old buddy Harv at the gun range. I pulled in at ten-twenty on Tuesday morning, the seventh. There were seven cars in the lot, so they weren't busy. I was hoping Harv might be due for a coffee break.

I entered and bypassed the sales counter. I saw Harvey at a distance and waved. He gave me the one-moment sign, and I moved to a sitting area behind the shooters.

I stood as Harvey approached, "Happy New Year to you, Harvey. How were your holidays?"

"They be alright Mr. Frank, thanks. Where's your gun?"

"Not shooting today, Harv. I thought I could buy you a cup of coffee."

"We got free coffee here. Just let me get Mr. Atkins set up and I'll be right with you."

When he returned, he led me into a small room with a Keurig machine, a selection of pods, and a box that once contained a dozen donuts; three remained. We each made our coffee, and Harv selected a glazed donut. We sat at the empty table; no one else was in the room.

"What's on your mind, Mr. Frank?"

I handed Harvey a rolled-up one-hundred-dollar bill and said, "What can you tell me about Anton Mitchell?"

"You don't need to pay me for that kind of question, Mr. Frank. You ain't with the PO-Leece, are you, Mr. Frank?"

"Do I look like I'm with the PO-Leece, Harv? Perhaps you know Mitchell was once married to Tawana Chaplin. I was dating Tawana. I'm doing a little investigating on my own."

"The woman that got killed? Mercy! So sorry about that, Mr. Frank. We don't have a lot of killings here on the Island. This one's big news, you know, one of our own. I can tell you for a fact that Mitchell is a son-of-a-bitch, Mr. Frank. The rest of what I can tell you are rumors."

"I'll take rumors, Harv."

"I heard that he and Tyrone are selling drugs to the kids hanging around at Coligny Beach at night. And it ain't just weed, but some of that real bad stuff, fentanyl or whatever."

"Where's he getting the stuff?"

"Another rumor is some big drug guy brings a boat into Station Beach 18 on Sullivan's Island, close to Fort Sumter. Then distributors from as far away as Wilmington and Jacksonville come by boat to buy and sell. I got no idea who else is involved, so help me.

An even better rumor is he's involved with an online prostitution ring catering to the golf groups that visit in the spring and fall."

"Mitchell got a boat?"

"He does. Keeps it down at Palmetto Bay Marina. You'll know if because it's all wood; about twenty feet."

"You've earned every penny of my gratuity, Harv. This is all very helpful. I'll let you get back to work."

"Mr. Frank, we ain't never had this conversation, please."

"What conversation, Harv?"

I wasn't sure of my next step. But I owed it to Tawana, and it would get me off the suspect list.

Chapter 27

Detective Vernon Brown walked into the offices of The O'Connor Group at Liberty Place in Philadelphia. The receptionist summoned Mr. O'Connor's personal assistant, Michele, and she led him back to the executive suite.

"May I offer you coffee, Detective?"

"That would be great, Michele. black is fine, thank you."

Brown looked around the executive suite and admired the furnishings and artwork. *No expense spared here*, he thought. Michele returned with his coffee, served in fine China. No paper cups back here.

"Mr. O'Connor is trying to wrap up this call. He shouldn't be long."

And he wasn't. O'Connor stepped out of his office and greeted Brown with a warm smile and handshake. He led him into the office and pointed towards the alcove near the fireplace. The high-end and expensive decor carried into this room.

"Have a seat, detective. I see Michele offered you coffee; should you want anything else, please let me know."

O'Connor was six-foot-two, fair complexion, lean, and short brown hair. A *bit too perfect*, Brown thought to himself. And he had a grin that made you think he knew something you did not.

"I'm fine, Mr. O'Connor, and thanks for seeing me on short notice. And thanks for the employee list you provided me. We'll discuss that in a bit, but could you give me an overview of The O'Connor Group, please?"

"Sure, and please call me Sean, or JR. My dad was a visionary in the financial services field. Educated as an accountant, he saw that the financial services world was changing. Until that time, accountants did taxes, stock brokers sold investments, and insurance people sold insurance. Banking and insurance laws were changing, and my dad sensed affluent people would prefer one advisor to look after their financial world.

"He formed tax, investment, and insurance divisions, and had his accounting client base.

"There was always a focus on affluent individuals, business owners, and professionals. He always said, *go where the money is.* He grew the business to where it is today."

"Very interesting. And you joined the first out of college?

"I went to St. Joseph's and then got an MBA from Wharton, but yes, this is the only job I have ever had."

"Your dad retired?"

"My dad never retired. He spent much more time pursuing other interests and traveling, but make no mistake, my dad was always on call to make big decisions."

"I've heard that your dad could be a tough boss. Any of the current or former employees strike you as capable or disgruntled enough to kill him?"

"I thought you said it was a robbery?"

"Or made to look like a robbery. We need to consider all the possibilities."

"My dad was a tough task-master and a perfectionist. So yes, there were some number of employees who left kicking and screaming, but I doubt one of them would murder him."

"We are cross-checking this list against the license plates we captured and will see if there is any crossover. The next question is hard to ask, but our tech specialists uncovered several anonymous emails extorting money to keep their relationship a secret. What can you tell me about that side of his life?"

"Nothing detective. I knew my dad was a philanderer, but we never discussed it and I'm not comfortable discussing it now. Are we done here?"

"Do you think your mother was aware of his philandering?"

"I couldn't say." O'Connor stood, indicating the meeting was over.

Brown stood, shook hands, and thanked him again for his time.

Chapter 28

The next morning, Detective Brown updated his partner, Roberta Rumson, and then headed to Captain Webster's office.

"Morning Cap; got a minute or two?"

"Always, Vern, especially if you arrested O'Connor's murderer."

"Not yet." He entered and sat in front of Captain Eleanor Webster.

"OK, whatta ya got, Vern?"

"Couple of things. First, we have these anonymous emails from a woman who was extorting money from O'Connor. If O'Connor was pushing back and threatening to come to us, she would have a motive.

"O'Connor's son claims he knew his dad was cheating on his mother but knew no details, and didn't want any, *see no evil*... Right now, this is priority one, and I have to hope the tech guys can find something. But it might warrant interviewing some employees at O'Connor. Someone may know about his secret affairs.

"Second, and I do not know what to do with this, we had one match of a former employee CCTV caught his plate the night of the murder. A guy by the name of Lazarus. Worked there from 1985 until 1992. He's seventy-eight-years-old, retired, and living in South Carolina. Hilton Head, to be exact. His car has a South Carolina plate."

"So you think, Vern, the seventy-eight-year-old guy, waits thirty-two years, drives up to Philadelphia, goes to a basketball game, kills his old boss, and drives back to Hilton Head? Is that about, right?"

"I told you I didn't know what to do about it. When we spoke with him, he said he was a St. Joe alumni and often attended basketball games when he was in the area. Said he learned about the murder the next day. No one asked him about Sean O'Connor."

"Please don't tell me you want me to allow you a week in Hilton Head to pursue Mr. Lazarus."

"The thought had entered my mind. You know, look this dude in the eye."

"Nice try, Vern. Call him and see what you can shake out. I would need a lot more to authorize your vaycay."

"Will do, Cap. Thanks."

***

I got home from the golf course at five-thirty after playing nine holes. I noticed a call came in an hour ago but went straight to voicemail. I showered, made myself a drink, and listened to the message:

"HELLO, MR. LAZARUS. THIS IS DETECTIVE VERNON BROWN AT THE PHILADELPHIA POLICE DEPARTMENT. I KNOW YOU SPOKE WITH THE DEPARTMENT A COUPLE OF WEEKS AGO, BUT I HAD A COUPLE OF MORE QUESTIONS. PLEASE RETURN MY CALL AS SOON AS POSSIBLE."

I wonder about this. At least I'll be able to talk to Detective Brown. But it can wait until the morning.

After writing from eight until ten, I made my second cup of coffee and went out to the patio. I dialed Brown's cellphone.

"Detective Brown. Good morning Mr. Lazarus. Thanks for returning my call."

"You're welcome, I'm sure. But first, may I ask, are you really Vernon Brown? You may not know this, but I created you in my first novel, *THE MURDER GAMBIT*."

"I'm sure my parents would like to discuss this with you, but I am Vernon Brown. As I said in my message, I have a couple of more questions for you. I have since learned that you worked at The O'Connor Group. You did not mention that on the earlier call."

"I do not recall, but if your people asked me, I would have told them I worked for O'Connor."

"Did you leave there on good terms?"

"I doubt, detective, that anyone leaves there on good terms. I'm don't know how many others you have spoken with, but Mr. O'Connor was not a very pleasant person."

"Did he owe you money, or vice versa?"

No, but the final straw was about money. Isn't it always? I wanted more for my salespeople, who were being wooed by a competitor. When he refused, I and my salespeople left to join another insurance company. End of story."

"Did you see him again?"

"We did not travel in the same social settings, but I may have seen him at an industry meeting or two after that. I have not seen him in twenty-five years.

"I sent a note to his wife, Chrissy, after his death, and received a nice reply."

"Did you know anything about his extra-marital activity?"

"It fits his profile, but I knew nothing specific."

"What do you mean by *it fits his profile?*"

"Wealthy, powerful, narcissist."

"Can you tell me anything about his son, Sean Jr?"

"I left before Junior came into the business, so I knew him only slightly when he was a teenager. I heard later he was much like his father, but with a more polished exterior."

"Anything else you can think of that might help us find the murderer?"

"I'm a murder mystery writer, detective. Follow the money, they always say. And you should read THE MURDER GAMBIT. You may learn quite a bit about yourself."

"I'll consider that, Mr. Lazarus. Thank you for your time and have a good day, sir."

"You too, Detective Brown."

I think I did well. He seems focused on those *other women*, and I suspect that will keep him busy.

Chapter 29

I had a couple of options.

I could, and probably should, dump Tawana's murder and Anton Mitchell on that Detective Hampton of the Beaufort County Detective Office. He would see how cooperative I was and forget about me.

More likely he'd think I was tossing him a red herring to direct him away from me. Why are they always so cynical?

But if I continue investigating on my own, I can always take it to the police if I learn more.

What the hell do I know about investigating a murder? When I am writing about murders, I make this shit up. Whatever Monk did in last week's episode is a good start for me. But this is real life.

I at least have a suspect, but I'm uncertain he had a motive to kill Tawana. They divorced ten years ago, so why now? Tawana had rarely spoken to me about him. Did she know he was still in touch with her brother? Did she know about the drugs?

I wanted to see if I could find this boat Harvey had told me about.

The Palmetto Bay Marina is one of four public marinas on Hilton Head and is best known for the Sunrise Cafe. It sits on the Broad Creek, a waterway that divides Hilton Head into north and south, or is it east and west?

After breakfast at Sunrise Cafe, I walk over to the marina. It was about as cold as it gets on Hilton Head in the winter; forty-three degrees, but with the wind coming off the water, it felt like zero to me. I am in shorts, of course, but swapped out my Eagles sweatshirt for a Hilton Head one to look more like a tourist.

The marina is the smallest of the four, and it was easy to spot. I'm not a boat guy, so Harvey's description of an all-wood boat would have to suffice. It stood out in the marina. Anton Mitchell was good enough to name it The MitchellBoat, a play on the words of his last name and the famous Mitchelville neighborhood on the Island.

I had the forethought to bring the tracking device I had recovered from Sean O'Connor's car the night of the murder. It still had plenty of life in it. My thought was to place it on Mitchell's boat and then track it to see when headed north toward Charleston. Truth be told, I did not know how long it might take the boat to get to Sullivan's Island, but I knew it would take me two hours by car, allowing for only one pee stop.

There was little to no activity in the marina as they were not hauling in fish at this marina. No pleasure boats, jet skis, Dolphin Tours, or Fishing Charters are venturing out today.

One of the medium-sized yachts was being power-cleaned by a two-person work crew, but they seemed oblivious to me. I casually walked out to the pier to Mitchell's boat and leaned on it, glancing to make sure the cleaning crew had not shifted their attention to me. They had not, and I placed the tracker under the inside railing of the boat.

I remained there for another two minutes, then nonchalantly sauntered back to the dock.

I had lost nothing of my sleuthing prowess in the last month. Since it felt like it might snow, I high-tailed it home.

Chapter 30

I am questioning my idea to track this boat.

I thought I would wait until it took off after dark and headed north towards Sullivan's Island. I packed a bag with a puffy vest, black knit cap, thermos, binoculars, telescopic lens for my iPhone, snacks, a book, toilet paper, and several shots of 5-Hour Energy.

The first week, in mid-January, the boat left the marina three times: once north to Skull Creek, once to South Beach, and the other to Daufuskie Island. I couldn't jump in my car every time the boat moved, and I could never get over to Daufuskie, period.

But on Thursday night, the sixteenth, I got a beep at seven-fifteen: the boat was on the move. This was the first time it moved at night since I placed the tracer.

Even though I still had time, I prepared to go hunting. It would take fifteen to twenty minutes for the boat to clear the Broad Creek, and if it went south there, another ten minutes to clear South Beach. If it continued south, it was toward Tybee Island and

Savannah. But a northeast direction could suggest Sullivan Island and time for me to go.

And it's go-time for me. The boat took the northeast direction. I double-checked everything and took off. It was five before eight. I'd never make it home for bedtime; *I'm fucking nuts*, I thought to myself.

It was still fifty-five degrees, but cloudy, and only a sliver of a moon. But the temps would drop another ten degrees for sure, and I was glad I replaced my shorts with jeans.

Unlike the crows and boats, cars did not have a direct route to Sullivan's Island. I thus had to drive twenty miles northwest before I could head northeast to get around the Colleton River, and then the Port Royal Sound. Then north again to get around the sea islands and inland waterways.

After taking Route seventeen to bypass Charleston, I headed through Mt. Pleasant and decided I was close enough to fill my thermos with hot coffee. I stopped at Parker's Kitchen, the Lowcountry's Wawa, and three sixteen-ounce cups filled the thermos. I added a couple of TastyKakes to the bag and finished the drive to Sullivan's Island.

There was no marina at Station 18 Beach, only a few docks for small to medium-sized boats. Again, in mid-January, there were only two small boats moored there. I parked on the street by the elementary school, a short walk to the beach, and followed the BEACH ACCESS sign. There was no boardwalk or promenade, but where the beach started, they built a small, covered deck with a couple of benches and two telescopes.

This presented me with another option. I thought I would sneak and camp out in the tall seagrass as close to the dock as I could get. I noticed three dog-walkers on the beach and two allowed the dogs to run free. If I attracted the dogs, I wasn't certain what I would tell the owners what I was doing in the grass.

I decided sitting on that deck pretending to be a stargazer might be safer.

It was five after ten and forty-six degrees. I set up camp and had my binoculars and iPhone at the ready. I put on the knit cap and poured myself a cup of coffee.

Looking through the binoculars, I could see the dock. A third boat had docked, about twice the size of the prior two. It looked like three people were on it, and now the other two boats were lit and each had two occupants. Mitchell's was not one of them.

I picked up my iPhone. With the telephoto lens, I could see closer with this than the binoculars. The larger boat's name was *Nauti Buoy*.

I did not know if these were part of the drug thing or were three boats parked at a dock. I knew the larger one had arrived after I got here, a bit late for sightseeing.

I got my answer soon enough. As if receiving a signal, the occupants of the two smaller craft exited their boats and climbed aboard the *Nauti Buoy*. One of the three on the *Nauti* was a black woman, and two of the five men were black. All seven exchanged greetings, and one guy stood out as the leader of the group.

He was white, tall, bald, and athletic-looking. He poured drinks, and they all toasted something or someone. I got the best pictures I could, but facial details were not very good.

"Get any good shots?" a man asked, and I jumped.

"Shit, you scared the beegeebers out of me. You shouldn't do that."

The seventy-ish man had leashed his dog and was now sniffing my jeans.

"Sorry, didn't mean to scare you. Cold out here for stargazing."

"A bit, but I was hoping the clouds would lift, and I'd get more stars out here. When I saw the boats, I thought I'd get a picture of them."

"You picked the right night; they're here almost every Thursday. Three or four more boats might still come later. If I was a more suspicious guy, I might think something sinister was transpiring. If you stay long enough, you'll see them taking boxes off the larger boat. Probably just peaches, huh?"

"Geez, I don't know. I don't want to get involved in any of that. Perhaps I should get going."

"Speaking of, I got to get going myself. Good luck catching some stars."

"Hey, thanks. Nice chatting with you."

This was now getting interesting. It was time for a second cup of coffee and a Butterscotch Krimpet.

They were hugging again, possibly suggesting the drinking was over. Back on deck, each person picked up a box the size you might put folders or bottles in. Taking out the camera, I could see the boxes labeled *PRODUCE FROM WAGNER FARMS.* They carried them to their respective boats, then returned to the *Nauti* and repeated with more boxes. I took more pictures.

The two small boats took off, both heading north. Almost as if it had been waiting for those two to leave, another boat approached the dock. There was no need to see the name on this boat. It was Anton Mitchell's woody. As it pulled into the dock, Tyrone Chaplin jumped out and secured the tie-lines to the dock.

They walked over to the *Nauti Buoy* and exchanged greetings. There was no hugging, no drinking; just handshakes and what appeared to be a handing over of an envelope. After that, Anton and Tyrone came on deck and picked up a box each, and they departed. The entire docking, exchange, and departure took fifteen minutes.

I had no evidence this was a drug deal, and other than Anton and Tyrone, I did not know who the other participants were, but I didn't care. I'm not the DEA. I had what I came for.

Eleven thirty at night. And people say I'm not a swinger. I showed them. I returned to my car and decided on one of those power naps my daughter, Laura, told me about.

Two hours later, I woke up needing to take a pee. After that, I poured myself another cup of coffee and drove back to Hilton Head.

Chapter 31

After speaking with me, Brown asked his partner to huddle in the conference room.

Roberta Rumson was a thirty-four-year-old black woman who fast-tracked to the detective position. Two years ago, Captain Webster asked Brown if he would accept her as a partner after arresting his previous partner for removing drugs for personal use at a drug sting.

After deliberation and discussion with his wife, Ronnie, Brown agreed to mentor Rumson. So far, so good.

"We ain't got shit after a month, Robbie. The captain is not happy. The only lead we have is this anonymous blackmailer. Have we been able to find any money going to her from O'Connor or through the business?"

"The forensic team has been through their books three times now, Vern, and came up with nothing. I'm sure he had sense enough not to handle it through the company. But there were no red flags in his personal accounts either. Even if this woman X was his only dalliance, he's done a good job hiding any payments to her. The captain wasn't excited about our Hilton Head suspect?"

"There's no Shrimp and Grits in our immediate future, Rob. Get someone to look into anyone and everyone, O'Connor, senior or junior. communicated within the last year. You and I need to visit the widow again. I'll call her and see if we can meet her this afternoon."

"On it, Vern."

***

Brown and Rumson had a two o'clock appointment with Christine O'Connor at her home in Swarthmore.

Swarthmore was the diamond in the rough in suburban Philadelphia's Delaware County. A county known for its blue-collar, lunch-pail inhabitants, Swarthmore has about seven thousand residents. Few carried a lunch pail to work.

In deference to its namesake Swarthmore College, the borough named half of their streets after Eastern colleges and universities.

The O'Connor property was near the intersection of Dartmouth and Amherst Avenues. The gate was open, expecting the detectives.

Brown parked in the circular drive behind a Mercedes GLS 450.

Very little is new in Swarthmore, and staring at the huge Tudor-style home, Brown dated the home to the 1930s-1940s. "We're not in Kansas anymore, Dorothy," Rumson said.

"Welcome to the land of the rich and famous, Ronnie."

Brown rang the doorbell and Mrs. O'Connor herself opened the door. "Mrs. O'Connor? I'm Detective Brown and my partner, Detective Rumson," both flashing their badges as they stepped into the foyer.

"Yes, I believe we met after my husband's death. Please come in."

She led them into a sitting room off the foyer. It was a small, comfortable room, and they took seats on the loveseat, leaving the single chair for Mrs. O'Connor.

"Thanks for seeing us on short notice, Mrs. O'Connor. Your home here is lovely. Have you been here long?"

"Almost thirty-five years now. But I'm not certain for how much longer. It might be time for me to downsize. There are several new 55+ communities in the area. Now, how can I help you?"

Brown continued, "We have made little progress in finding your husband's murderer and wanted to talk to you further. While this very well could be a random robbery gone bad, we must also consider the possibility it was not random, that someone wanted to kill your husband."

"oh my. Who would do such a thing?"

"That's where we hope you might help. Your son has provided me with a list of current and former employees. We have interviewed or spoken with many and don't have any suspects from that group, except one guy named Lazarus, who worked for your husband many years ago and was at the basketball game that night. Ring any bells?"

"Frank Lazarus, of course. I received a pleasant note from him after Sean's death. You do not suspect Frank, do you?"

"Not really, but I had to ask. Can you think of anyone who might have wanted to harm your husband?"

"I do not know many of his employees at all, current or former. I only knew Frank thirty years ago, when the firm was much smaller. We had social events that I attended. And Sean talked little about his employees."

"You'll have to forgive me, but I must ask a personal and sensitive question. We have identified one suspect who seems to have been blackmailing your husband. We do not have any details, but might you know of anything he might have been involved with that could lead to his being blackmailed?"

Brown noticed an obvious tell on her face and waited to hear her answer.

"Detective, I'll confirm that my husband was unfaithful, but I do not know how many women or any details. It was something I chose to ignore, and I hoped it would not cause me or my family embarrassment. He seems to have been discreet."

"It was apparent that he paid at least this one woman for her silence, but we cannot find any record of payments from his business or personal accounts. Might you be aware of any other hidden accounts?"

"I do not. I have met with our attorney regarding my husband's Will and Estate, but he mentioned nothing surprising or unusual."

"May I have his name, please? And might there be anyone else your husband would confide in or use for such private matters?

"Bill McIntyre is our personal estate attorney. Jim Reynolds at Isdaner & Company is our personal and company accountant. The only other person I can think of is Eli Kapustin. I'm not certain just what Eli does, but I am quite certain he handles our investments and other confidential matters for Sean. He'd be a good one to talk to. I'll get you their phone numbers."

"That would be helpful, thank you. Robbie, anything else?"

"Have you heard from anyone else claiming your husband owed them money? It's not unusual for scammers to come after wealthy widows."

"No, fortunately, but I'll be on the lookout for those. Now, let me get you those phone numbers."

They all stood, and Mrs. O'Connor went upstairs while Brown and Rumson returned to the foyer. Mrs. O'Connor returned and handed Brown a piece of paper.

"I hope this helps. Call if I can be of any further assistance."

"We will, Mrs. O'Connor, and thank you again for your time."

"Takeaways, Ronnie?"

"She knew of his philandering. Does that make her a suspect? Perhaps she or the family got embarrassed?"

"Possibly. This Kapustin guy sounds interesting. I'll call him in the morning."

Chapter 32

Robbie Rumson beat Vernon Brown into the office the next morning and had coffee waiting when Brown showed up with a box of Dunkin Donuts.

"So how is James McNeil?" Rumson asked.

"Am I that predictable? And James is fine, thank you. I was thinking it might be best to surprise Mr. Kapustin this morning. You OK with that?"

"Sure, but he's seventy-eight; you sure he goes into the office every day?"

"I'm not, but if he's not, we'll reschedule. But you know I prefer to catch people off-guard when possible. If he's not there, we're no worse off. We'll leave here at nine-thirty. When we are in town, perhaps we should pop in on the accountant. I know we have reviewed their financial statements, but perhaps if we have a chat, he'll give us something."

"Can't hurt. We are getting desperate."

"Meanwhile, I'm going to read up on this Eli Kapustin."

From the station at 55th & Pine Streets, there were few options for driving into the city. Brown went over to Walnut Street and turned east toward Center City.

"Learn much about Kapustin?"

"More about him personally than professionally. He's a seventy-eight-year-old, wealthy, and active in Jewish charities and causes. He's the son of Holocaust survivors. Law Degree from Penn, MBA from Wharton, a Certified Financial Planner, and Registered Investment Advisor. His firm is Elk Advisors.

"But, ELK Advisors is a phantom!

"They have no website or telephone listing and do not advertise. They are a referral-only advisory firm. Even the word *ADVISORS* is an anomaly. No one is quite certain about what they advise. I hope we can get a peek behind the curtain."

They turned north onto 18th Street and up to Arch Street, parking in the first *LOADING ZONE* they found.

ELK Advisors occupied twenty-five percent of the fifth floor in the Comcast Center, the World Headquarters of the Comcast Corporation. Comcast occupied ninety percent of the fifty-eight-story building.

The other ten percent of the occupants were there at the invite of Comcast, and that Kapustin was a friend of the late Ralph Roberts, Comcast's Founder.

After locating the Elk Advisor's office, Brown approached the receptionist. "Good morning. I'm Detective Brown and this is Detective Rumson of the Philly PD," showing their badges. "Is Mr. Kapustin available?"

"Which Mr. Kapustin? There are two, Eli and his son, David."

"Eli, please."

"Do you have an appointment, detective?"

"We do not."

"Please have a seat. I'll see if he's available."

Brown perused the offices of ELK Advisors. Everything was first class, but not extravagant or pretentious. Hardwood floors with area carpets, mahogany furniture, Philadelphia and Israeli artwork.

There were also pictures of Eli Kapustin with Former Mayor and Governor Ed Rendell, Ralph and Suzanne Roberts, and President Trachtman. Brown found them impressive.

Five minutes later, a tall, attractive, red-haired woman approached them and said, "Detectives, I'm Myra Feldman, Mr. Kapustin's Executive Assistant. Please follow me. Mr. Kapustin is finishing a meeting and should not be much longer. May I offer you something to drink?"

She showed them to chairs in an alcove outside of Kapustin's office.

"Not for me, thanks. Ronnie?"

"I'm fine too."

Two minutes later, a man and woman, who appeared to be employees, left the office and a minute later, Eli Kapustin emerged with a big smile on his face and hand extended. "Welcome, detectives. Sorry to keep you waiting. Did my parking tickets exceed the threshold again?"

"Nothing quite so serious, sir, and thank you for making time for us."

Kapustin led them into his office and showed them seats by the fireplace. Brown noticed more pictures of Kapustin with Israeli and US leaders, and awards from various civic and charitable organizations.

"What is on your mind, detectives?"

"We were speaking with Mrs. O'Connor and she mentioned you as a good friend and advisor to her late husband. We hoped you might fill us in on O'Connor's private life more than she could do."

"I'm not certain I can do that, but Sean was a good friend. I thought his murder was a random robbery; was I misinformed?"

"That is quite possible, but we are also considering it might have been personal. Can you think of anyone who might wish him harmed?"

"Tough to say, detective. Sean O'Connor was not always pleasant and had the proverbial Irish temper that got the best of him. I understand he could be a difficult boss, father, and husband. But I am not certain I could be more specific. I was not involved with his business."

"Off subject; exactly what does ELK Advisors do?"

"A little of everything. We are investment advisors and handle the accounts of wealthy individuals.

"We also invest pension and 401(k) funds for select corporations. We can be dealmakers, putting some investors together for mutual benefit, or perhaps, forming a non-profit 503(C) Corporation.

"We even pay the bills for a few clients.

"I also like to think we can be problem-solvers, in IRS disputes, mergers, acquisitions, and corporate takeovers. I encourage my friends to call me whenever they have a problem."

"And for Sean O'Connor?"

"Without violating client confidentiality, detective, I can confirm we did business with Sean. I would need a warrant or subpoena to disclose more."

"I understand. Can you tell me about his personal life? We learned he had one or more extramarital affairs."

"Since Sean's wife, Christine, called me last night and told me she confirmed that to you, I can tell you Sean did whore around on more than one occasion." Looking at his watch, he said, "I have a call at ten-thirty. Is that about it?"

"For now, but I think we'll be back with a search warrant. Again, we appreciate your time. Thank you, Mr. Kapustin."

They stood, and Kapustin opened the door for them.

Waiting for the elevator, Rumson asked, "Do we have sufficient *probable cause* for a warrant?"

"I'm not certain, Robbie. We'll see what the DA thinks. We have evidence that O'Connor was being blackmailed, can show he made no payments from any of his known accounts, and Kapustin was a fixer, who may have helped fix this problem. I think it's 50/50."

Chapter 33

The next morning, I once again struggled with what to do next.

I've now identified four boats and have pictures of nine participants. I consider this the good news.

The not-as-good news is I have no evidence of drugs, and other than Tyrone and Anton, I do not know the other seven.

I'm thinking the best I can do is identify the seven and then turn it over to the Beaufort County Sherriff. But other than Harvey, I don't know who might identify these people. I know Harvey is hoping never to see me again. I know several bartenders who have been on Hilton Head for some time. Bartenders know everyone.

Then I have a better idea. The Coastal Discovery Museum is a facility with maps, pictures, and artifacts detailing the history of Hilton Head and the Gullah families that played such a huge part in it.

Even better, the volunteers were always sweet old ladies who loved to talk about the Island's history and people. And they know even more people than the bartenders.

It was one of those winter days on the Island we dream about. Sunny, with little or no wind, and the temperature expected to get to the low seventies. I planned to go to the beach for an hour or two this afternoon, so I went straight to the CDM. The bus for the Gullah Bus Tour was sitting there, most likely waiting for the ten-thirty tour. I took the bus tour last year, and it visited the original Gullah neighborhoods, churches, schools, and cemeteries on the Island.

Is it possible my driver, Carl, was taking this bus out? I think he liked me. I asked a lot of questions and entertained him and the other passengers. Lo-and-behold, he was standing at the entrance to the museum chatting with a volunteer.

I approached. "Excuse me, your name is Carl, isn't it?"

"It is. Do I know you?"

"I took your tour last year. My name is Frank. Certainly, you could not have forgotten me already."

"I remember you now, Mr. Frank; funny, white dude."

"I'm white? I hadn't noticed."

"You see, you are still funny."

"I've got better stuff than that, Carl. Are you taking the ten-thirty tour out?"

"I am. You want to come? It's half off for prior customers."

"Perhaps another time, but might I ask you a couple of questions, Carl? It won't take long." I led him towards an empty exhibit room for some privacy while I searched my iPhone for the pictures.

"I was taking some random pictures the other night and I'm trying to identify the people, see if I have anyone famous. Would you take a peek, please?"

I enlarged the pictures as much as I could without sacrificing the detail. I knew they weren't great, but it was the best I could do. Carl stared at the first picture, shaking his head in the negative. I showed the next picture, and Carl took the phone from me for closer scrutiny. After a moment, he said, "This here woman, that's Juanita White. She's a Ward leader on the Town Council. And the white guy with her looks familiar, but I don't know his name."

Carl flipped to the next picture.

"And this fellow here; he's a guy by the name of Anton Mitchell. A bad actor, if you ask me. Were these two together? That would seem unlikely to me."

"Nah, as I said, they were random. You've been very helpful, Carl. Thank you for your time." I handed him a twenty-dollar bill for his time. He was grateful.

"You're welcome, Mr. Frank. Don't forget the discount for the next tour."

"I'll check my calendar as soon as I get home. Thanks again, Carl."

A Town Council member? Shit. I got my own IslandGate right here in the Lowcountry.

Chapter 34

Philadelphia District Attorney David Kasper desperately wanted the police to find O'Connor's murderer.

Not convinced of Detective Brown's *probable cause* justification, he asked his ADA, Michelle Pugh, to take the warrant request to a friendly judge, Philomena Rossi. After a couple of perfunctory questions, Rossi signed the warrant.

A week later, Brown and Rumson were meeting with Captain Webster, each looking at the copy of the initial forensic audit.

AUDIT REPORT TO BROWN AFTER COURT ORDER

Date of Report: January 15, 2025

Per the court order to audit any accounts that the deceased, Sean O'Connor, may have held with ELK Advisors, the undersigned submit:

O'Connor established an Investment Account with ELK Advisors in 1989. Per the order, we limited our focus to 2019 through 2024. Eli Kapustin and David Kapustin had discretionary powers on the account.

The account's diversified holdings included common stocks and other traded securities, REITs, private LLCs, Cryptocurrencies, artwork, and precious metals. As of 12/31/2024, the balance was $34,650,129. Attached is Exhibit I, a complete list of the holdings as of 12/31/24.

Deposits to the account come from various sources: The O'Connor Group's operating account, O'Connor Properties, LLC, O'Connor Java Shops, LLC, and SPO Collectibles, LLC.

For the last five years, they transferred $100,000 a month to an account in the Cayman Islands' First National Bank. The account is in the name of ELKSPO Operating account. ELKSPO is a corporation organized in the Cayman Islands. The officers and signatories are David Kapustin and Myra Feldman. The balance in this account, as of 12/31/2024 was $3,473,000.

The account made disbursements to various individuals and entities with supporting invoices for SERVICES RENDERED, GOODS DELIVERED PER ORDER, CONSULTING SERVICES, AND PER MANIFEST. A complete list is attached as Exhibit II.

Further examination of said accounts will be performed at the court's pleasure.

"It seems to me are looking at potential money laundering, shell companies, secret or illegal payments to unidentified parties, and who knows what else. I believe we are close to needing the FBI's involvement; what do you both think?"

Brown knew Rumson was waiting for him to reply first. "I don't disagree, Cap, but this is still our murder investigation. Before doing that, I'd like to meet with Kapustin again and see if he'll give up the mystery woman. She's still our only suspect, and I'd like to interview her. Ideally, we nail her for the murder and let the FBI take over whatever the hell the rest of this might be. Make sense? Robbie?"

"Agree. O'Connor's murder is our priority. And perhaps this woman can add to the story and give us more names."

Captain Webster agrees. "I'm good with this, but keep it on a fast track. See if you can meet with Kapustin yet today. Keep me informed. Good work, guys."

***

At two o'clock, the assistant escorted Brown and Rumson into Eli Kapustin's office. Myra Feldman was sitting at the conference table.

"Good afternoon, detectives. I believe you have met Myra before. My son is out of the country and thus, will not be joining us. Please have a seat."

"Yes, we met on our last visit. Good to see you again, Ms. Feldman. Thank you for seeing us on short notice."

"You know, we wish to help you find Mr. O'Connor's murderer. How can we help?"

Removing the audit report from his attaché, Brown said, "Our preliminary audit reveals a business account in the Cayman Islands First National Bank, and your son and Ms. Feldman are the signatories.

"Since the deposits come from Mr. O'Connor's investment account here at ELK Advisors, we assume they are related."

Kapustin nodded to Feldman to respond. "That is correct, detective. Many years ago, Mr. O'Connor requested we establish a company for him in the Caymans. He authorized transfers from his investment account and provided others to wire deposits to this account.

"He also established some automatic payments and provided a list of vendors we could pay upon receipt of invoices. If there was ever any question about an invoice, we referred it to Mr. O'Connor or his son."

"Thank you, Myra. I want to make this very clear, detectives. In these transactions, our firm was only performing a bookkeeping function for Mr. O'Connor. We were receiving deposits into the account and making payments only as authorized by the O'Connors. We are not involved with the businesses or individuals. I believe I mentioned to you we perform these services for several clients who prefer not to be involved with bookkeeping."

Brown handed Kapustin copies of emails to O'Connor from woman X. "Any idea who might have sent these to Mr. O'Connor?"

Kapustin glanced at them and slid them down to Feldman. He again gave her the nod to reply.

"Yes, I believe these must be from Lena Jovic. I would have to verify this, but about two years ago, Mr. O'Connor authorized us to pay her $10,000 a month. Back in October, he asked us to cease further payments. He did not provide any details, nor did we ask for any."

"Might you have an address for her?"

"I do not. We made the payments electronically. I can get you her bank information. I'm sure you can find her through that."

"Thank you. That would be helpful. Are there any other women like Jovic that were compensated for providing their services?"

"Not presently, but there have been over the years."

"Might you send me their names and account information when you have a chance?"

"Certainly."

They appeared to be done, and as they were preparing to leave, Rumson asked, "Are any such payments being made on behalf of Sean Junior?"

For the first time since they arrived, Kapustin looked flustered. He took a minute to ponder this before discreetly nodding to Feldman.

"Yes, detective. We are paying two such women. I will get you their names as well."

Brown said, "Thank you for your cooperation."

They stood and shook hands with Eli Kapustin and followed Myra Feldman out of his office.

Chapter 35

I had four bartenders I needed to speak to: Jimmy Calhoun at *Meet Street*, Becky Driscoll at *One Hot Mama's*, Rufus Cane at *Ruby Lee's,* and Shane Mc-Something at *Pool Bar Jim's*. It was a tough job, but someone had to do it.

I worked north to south, but I called Becky at *One Hot Mama's* and asked her to hold me a seat at the bar. She seemed pleased when I told her I'd be alone.

When Rufus Cane saw me enter, he poured me a Kettle One on the rocks. Rufus added one more name: besides Tyrone and Anton, he identified Walter Bridges from boat two.

Jimmy Calhoun gave me nothing, and I told him so. "You know Jimmy, you're worthless and if this continues, I might stop coming in here to abuse you."

"Oh. Please don't do that Laz. It would destroy my already low self-esteem."

I think Jimmy knew I was kidding because where else on the Island could I get chicken wings served on

French Fries with garlic parmesan sauce on top? Yeah, I'd be back.

I arrived at *One Hot Mama's* at six-fifteen. Unlike the summer when you wait an hour for a table, the place was only half full and the bar only had four others at it.

True to her word, Becky had a stool waiting for me at the end of the bar.

"Hey Laz; the usual?"

"You mean to eat or drink?"

"Both."

"Sure, Kettle One on the rocks with an orange slice, and the ribs and chicken combo, cornbread, and slaw. Slow down the food, though. I'm in no hurry. Thanks, Beck."

When she delivered the vodka, she said, "I was so sorry to hear about Tawana. Cops got any idea who did it?"

"If they do, they're not sharing it with me."

"You got something else on your mind?"

"Why would you think that?"

"I can't remember you ever calling for a reservation at the bar."

"You should be a detective, Beck."

"Yeah, but the pay is better here."

"True. If you have a minute, I took random pictures by the water and thought I'd try to identify the boaters. See if I captured anyone famous."

"If I buy you a second vodka, will you tell me the truth?"

"No. Are you going to look at these or not?" I slid my phone over to her. She perused them and then went back and studied them in greater detail.

"I assume you know Tawana's brother, Tyrone? The guy with him is a banger by the name of Anton. The only other guy I recognize is this white guy. His name is Alan Baxter, Big Al they call him. Real asshole. Some kind of bigwig with the County's Sherriff Department. You'd think he was the friggin governor the way he acts."

"Really? Very interesting, Beck. I appreciate this. I'll celebrate with another vodka, and you can put the food order in. Thanks."

After delivering my drink, Becky went off to tend to other customers, as the number at the bar had doubled. This left me to contemplate my life. I now have a Hilton Head Town Councilwoman and a guy in the County Sherriff's Office possibly involved in a drug ring. If this wasn't real life, I could write a novel using this. Those two detectives who interviewed me could work for this Baxter.

I was typing my notes into my iPhone when a server delivered my food order. Becky noticed and stopped back. "Everything looks OK?"

"Better than OK, Beck, but I'll have a *Yuengling* when it's convenient."

"You got it."

Left alone, could I stretch out my eating beyond seven minutes? Only if I read, so I opened my Kindle and read the *Philadelphia Inquirer* to see if there was any update on the O'Connor. Not finding any, I turned to coverage of the Eagles' Playoff game Sunday vs. their division rival Washington Commanders. Eagles were a -3.5 point favorite at home. I said a silent prayer for Saquon's knees.

Twenty minutes later, with only bones remaining, the server cleared my plates.

Becky came by, "Dessert?"

"I'll have to pass. Mama around by any chance?"

"Nah. Miss Orchid is doing some TV show somewhere. She's become a real diva, you know?"

"And for good reason. I'll take my check and get out of your hair."

"You're never in my hair, you know that, Laz. Come back soon."

"Will do, thanks again, Beck."

I doubled my usual tip. This investigation was abusing my retirement budget.

After three vodkas and a beer, I skipped Pool Bar Jim's and called for an Uber.

Chapter 36

Brown and Rumson now had a name and an address for their suspect, Lena Jovic. Not wanting to send her fleeing, they did not call for an appointment but arrived at The Locust Condominium on Rittenhouse Square in Philadelphia at ten o'clock on Friday morning.

The Locust was on the southeast corner of Rittenhouse Square. Built in 1942, Commonwealth Real Estate Investment Trust completely renovated it in 2013. They sold condominiums ranging in price from three to eight million, but the REIT retained ownership and rented twelve units, including 1107, to Lena Jovic.

After flashing badges to the security guard, they took the elevator to the eleventh floor. After ringing the bell at 1107, "Who's there?"

"Philadelphia Detective Brown," holding his badge up to the peephole.

A tall, twenty-something woman opened the door. Even in a gray sweatsuit, Nikes, and blond hair pinned up, Lena Jovic was an attractive woman.

Stepping into the condo and still holding their badges, Rumson said, "Ms. Jovic? I'm Detective Rumson and my partner, Detective Brown. We would like to ask you a few questions. May we come in?"

"What kinds of questions? Do you have a warrant?"

"Ma'am, we do not need a warrant to ask you questions."

Jovic stepped aside, allowing them to enter.

The condo was tastefully furnished, but not extravagantly. The northeast view was of the Philadelphia skyline and, beyond that, glimpses of New Jersey.

The floors were hardwood with imitation Asian area rugs. The limited artwork was of Philadelphia landmarks, Boathouse Row, the Art Museum, Independence Hall, and the Liberty Bell. There were no personal pictures. A seventy-two-inch Samsung TV dominated one wall.

Jovic did not offer coffee, but after they were all seated, she again asked, "You never answered, what kinds of questions do you have?"

Brown asked Rumson to take the lead, thinking it might put Jovic more at ease. It did not seem to work yet.

Rumson handed her copies of the emails. "We wanted to ask you about these, Ms. Jovic."

"What are these? I do not recognize them."

"That's how you want to play this, Lena? Would you rather have this conversation at our station? We know you sent these. You want to start again?"

"OK. Yes, they are from me to that bastard."

"Tell us about your relationship with Mr. O'Connor."

"Why do you want to know?"

"Someone killed Mr. O'Connor a month ago, Lena. I'm sure you are aware of that."

"I am aware of that, certainly. But I did not kill him. As you say here, *a dead man cannot pay you*."

"Your English is quite good, Lena. Where are you from, may I ask?"

"Serbia."

"We are still waiting to hear about your relationship with Mr. O'Connor."

"This is a long story and has nothing to do with his murder. I did not kill him. You must believe me."

"Let's hear the story first."

Lena Jovic lit a cigarette and took a deep breath. She had not told her story to anyone in the ten years she had been in this country. She feared the consequences but feared going to prison for murder even more.

"Ten years ago, a man by the name of Alek Vulic told me and three other women he could get us to the United States, get us good paying jobs, teach us English, a place to live, and get us started in a new life. It would cost us $10,000 each, but he would get paid once we had income from our jobs here. I had no reason to remain in Belgrade. I was not going to school, my mother had left us, and my father was a drunk and abuser of me.

"When we got to this country, a woman by the name of Jelena was in charge of us. We joined a group of fifteen other girls living in a small house somewhere in the city. Jelena was nice to us at first. We learned English, and they gave us clean clothes and fed us well. They implanted some type of device under our skin so they would always know where we were."

Brown interrupted her, "Do you know where you were held?"

"No, we never knew. We soon learned that we needed to have sex with men. They made us prostitutes. We walked the streets and went to bars to attract men. We never saw the money. A man by the name of Goric collected it.

"After a year or two, they took several of us to another location. We were further educated and taught how to eliminate our accents. They gave us much nicer clothes and our own small apartments. We were told we would now work by appointment and would deal with a better class of wealthier clients. But they were still pigs.

"We were now given money and had a certain amount of freedom to go out, see a movie, or eat a meal at a restaurant. Several of us were friendly and would do things together.

"Four years ago, Mr. O'Connor took me to his apartment for the first time. I assumed he was a client of Goric's. But six months later, Mr. O'Connor said that I would no longer be seeing other men. That I was to be exclusively his girlfriend. I moved here, and they gave me more clothes and more money. This is the end of the story."

"I don't think so, Lena. When did you start demanding payments from him?"

"I hated him, and I hated myself. I began planning to escape. I took pictures of us. I found out about his business and his family. By that time, I knew he also had another girl somewhere. Then, about two years ago, I showed him the pictures I had and told him of my plan to expose them unless he started paying me and allowed me to remain here."

"And then?"

"Three months ago, the payments stopped. I was told by Ms. Feldman that Mr. O'Connor ordered them to stop the payments. When I texted him, he wrote back,"Sue me."

"And then you began your threats?"

"Yes, but I never intended to kill him, and I did not, I swear."

Brown asked, "What is your immigration status, Lena?"

"I know little about that. They gave me what you call a green card. I get a new one every year or two. Do you need to see it?"

"Please." Brown took a picture with his phone.

"If I understand you, they brought you and the other young girls into this country illegally, kept captive, and forced into prostitution for almost ten years. Any idea how many girls or women in total?"

"I do not. I mentioned the fifteen when I first came, and three or four more would come every month or so. I do not know how many like me they moved to other locations."

"Lena, we are Philadelphia detectives, and it is our job to find Sean O'Connor's murderer. You are a suspect in that murder and must remain so. The district attorney may also charge you with extortion for these blackmail threats.

"But these other crimes are beyond our authority and we will refer this matter to other agencies, Homeland Security and the FBI. You are going to need an attorney, perhaps more than one. Your life could get much more complicated."

"All this because I let you into my home?"

"No, Lena. All this because you extorted and may have killed Sean O'Connor."

Brown stood, followed by Rumson, and they walked towards the door. Lena followed them.

"Rumson added, "We'll be in touch next week, Lena. Do as my partner suggested and get a lawyer."

On the way to the elevator, "Jesus H. Christ," Rumson exclaimed.

"And the horse He rode in on."

Chapter 37

"Hey, Charlie. Vernon Brown out here in West Philly. Remember me?"

"Sure, I remember you, Vern, but I'm holding my breath on why you're calling me."

Vernon Brown met Charles Bishop three years ago in *THE MURDER GAMBIT*. Bishop was Special Agent in Charge of the FBI's Philadelphia office. They collaborated to bring down a Russian hitman and a New York investment specialist, who were murdering senior citizens for profit.

"I'm hoping we might meet for lunch in the next day or so. Reading Terminal Market?"

"How about ten-thirty today? That should beat the lunch crowd at DiNici's and allow us to find a table."

"Good enough. See you there, and yes, Charlie, I got a big one for you."

When Brown arrived at the Reading Terminal Market, Bishop was holding a table close to DiNici's stand. At ten-thirty-five in the morning, there were ten people in line and three people sitting at the counter.

They greeted each other, and Brown said, "You hold the table, I'll get the sandwiches. Anything special on yours?"

"Horseradish on the side, and a diet Coke."

Non-Philadelphians always associate hoagies, cheesesteaks, soft pretzels, and maybe Tastycakes with Philadelphia, but Philadelphians add roast pork sandwiches with provolone and broccoli rabe to that list.

The first iteration of the sandwich was credited to Domenico Bucci, an immigrant from Abruzzo. According to the Philadelphia Inquirer, Bucci arrived through Ellis Island in 1918. By 1930, he opened a stand selling two sandwiches: a hoagie with meatballs and the original Philly pork sandwich. He named the place after his son, John, although the regulars knew it as the pork shack.

There are other places to find the sandwich, like DiNici's, in the Reading Market Terminal. The indoor market opened in 1893 and today serves as a food hall and shopping mall. DiNici's has made a name for themselves selling pork sandwiches stuffed with broccoli rabe, pork, and provolone.

Brown returned with his hands full, put the sandwiches down, and went back for more napkins that he was certain they would need.

"Thanks for the sandwich, Vern. You got a budget for this?"

"No, but I'll claim I gave it to a CI. How are things at the FBI?"

"As you would expect, never a dull moment. I'm certain, like the Philly PD, crime is a growth business."

"True, but mostly murders, domestics, burglaries, and drugs. Nice, wholesome crimes, not like that stuff y'all do."

With his mouth full, Bishop mumbled, "What do you have this time?"

Swallowing, Brown replied, "Did you hear about the murder last month of prominent businessman, Sean O'Connor?"

"That the one out at St. Joe's after a basketball game?"

"That's the one. Our only suspect is a woman who was blackmailing O'Connor. When we interviewed her, she told us a story of women brought to this country from Serbia and then forced into prostitution. It was hard to get a firm number on how many women were involved, but she said initially there were twenty, but there were always more coming and going. She said they elevated her and several others into call girls with private apartments, education, and clothes.

"She first thought O'Connor was just a John, but he later made her his exclusive, setting her up with an apartment in The Locust.

"We are only interested in her for O'Connor's murder, which she swears she did not do. Human trafficking and prostitution are above my pay grade."

"You still like her for the murder?"

"I'm believing her, even though that leaves me at square one."

"Immigration status?"

"She gave us a green card that turned out to be fake. I assume the other girls would be the same."

"In our always-efficient government, these crimes now fall into the domain of Homeland Security and ICE. Where is the woman now?"

"We did not hold her for the murder, so she may still be at The Locust. If I were her, I'd be in the wind, trying to get back to Belgrave."

"Give me what you've got, and I'll refer it to DHS. What is the next step in your murder investigation?"

"Other than threatening emails, we have no weapon, physical evidence, or witnesses, so we will keep digging for anything."

"Did you ever make it down to the Caymans to visit your buddy?"

"You're referring to Lamont McLamore, and he was James McNeil's buddy. But no, we've not visited him yet."

By eleven-forty-five, the line at DiNici's had grown to forty, and a couple was hovering over them, hoping for their table. They obliged them, and Brown and Bishop walked out to Twelfth Street where they went their separate ways.

Chapter 38

Sunday was like any other day for me, at least my writing in the morning.

I was at my desk doing so when my phone rang; it was Annie Chaplin.

"Good morning, Annie. How are you?"

"I didn't wake you, did I, Laz?"

"At nine o'clock? That'll be the day. No, just sitting here staring at my laptop waiting for brilliance to strike me. What's up?"

"Just wondering if you have any updates for me? And, I'll be on the Island next week visiting a friend. I thought we could get together for a drink or meal if you're available."

"Next weekend? I don't have this afternoon planned yet, let alone next weekend. So yes, let's get together. Let me know your schedule later in the week.

"Meanwhile, I have made some headway. Besides your Uncle Tyrone and your dad, I have identified two others in what appears to be a drug ring. I won't give you names over the phone, but one is on the Island's

Town Council and the other with the County Sherriff's office. This is making me nervous. I think I need to turn it over to someone, but I'm not certain just whom. We can discuss this when you are here. Anything new with you?"

"Not really. But I have a friend from high school I still see occasionally. His dad had a big job at the State Police. I could feel him out about his dad if you want to go that route. Let me know."

"That might be a place to start, Annie. Let me think about that and I'll text you. Otherwise, I'll plan to see you next weekend. Thanks for calling."

"Talk soon, bye."

***

Juanita White was a born worrywart, at least since she began accepting campaign donations and other favors from Major Alan Baxter.

White was a fifty-eight-year-old woman who was a fourth-generation Simmons family member on Hilton Head. She was serving her third term on Hilton Head's Town Council in Ward Four and had strong support from the Gullah community.

Baxter approached her six years ago, shortly after her husband died of lung cancer and money was tight.

All she had to do was support his agenda, an agenda he reminded her, she would most likely support, anyway. In return, he provided financial incentives that varied depending on the issue.

She thought most of Baxter's causes were to limit the use of Beaufort County Sheriff's Office's resources on Hilton Head. Traffic, parking, electric bikes, and trash disposal were just a few issues. Baxter preferred local police or private contractors to be used for such matters.

Yesterday, White got a call from Carl Mays, a neighbor who worked at the Gullah Bus Tours. He told her a guy showed him a picture of her with two guys, one white, on a boat. He was trying to find out who the people were in the picture. She called Alan Baxter and demanded they meet. She was on her way to Fish Haul Beach to meet him.

He was waiting on the bench overlooking the Port Royal Sound when she parked and joined him.

"Happy New Year, Juanita. A lovely January day it is here on Hilton Head. Something on your mind?"

"I told you on the phone, some guy has a picture of us on the boat. I assume it was from the other night up on Sullivan's Island. What are we going to do?"

"Does this photographer have a name?"

"The only name my source knew was Mr. Frank. He also had a picture of Mitchell and Chaplin."

"That very well could be a problem. Perhaps Mr. Frank was following Mitchell and Chaplin, looking into the murder of Mitchell's ex-wife. I'll never know why that hothead killed her. Getting involved with Mitchell was my mistake; one I need to fix. We need to identify Mr. Frank and determine what he's up to. Your source tell you anything else about him?"

"Only that he was an old, white guy. Oh yeah, he's a funny, old, white guy."

"Few of them on Hilton Head. Fortunately, it's winter and there are only about fifteen thousand of them. Get back to your guy and see if he can tell you anything more; description, car he was driving, where he lives, anything at all. Let me know what you find out.

"Meanwhile, try to relax, Juanita. There is no reason to suspect Mr. Frank has any interest in you or me. But you did the right thing in telling me. We need to make certain."

Baxter handed White an envelope as he stood and walked to his car. White remained sitting on the bench, staring across the water at nothing.

Chapter 39

I keep my phone on DO NOT DISTURB from ten p.m. until seven a.m., even though I'm not certain why. The only people who might call me in an emergency would be my kids, and they have access through the DND setting.

When I got up to pee at four-fifteen, I saw a message from Annie Chaplin she left at two-twenty this morning. Knowing that could not be good, I listened through her sobbing and sniffling:

SORRY TO WAKE YOU, LAZ, IT'S ME ANNIE. I'M ON MY WAY TO HILTON HEAD. THE POLICE CALLED ME. THEY SAID MY FATHER WAS KILLED LAST NIGHT. CALL ME WHEN YOU CAN.

I knew Annie had a strained relationship with her father, but in a moment like this, I empathized with her emotions and sadness.

I did not know Anton Mitchell well. Tawana and Annie did not see or speak about him very much. Tawana told me they divorced in 2015 when Annie was twelve years old. Despite being charming, handsome, and funny, he had few characteristics of a good husband and father. He was a chef wannabe, but always remained a cook at various places on the Island and nearby Bluffton. He lacked job stability, as his temper often got him in trouble.

He drank too much and began doing other drugs. He never had time for his daughter and often went out at night without explanation. When she suspected he was also dealing, that was the end for her.

After his divorce, he shared a trailer with Derrick Cohen in the Marshland neighborhood on the northern end of the Island. He refused to pay support and ignored the court order to make payments. Tawana dropped it so long as he remained out of their lives.

Her brother Tyrone told her a guy looking to move drugs on HHI recruited him and he thought that would be easy money.

Two years ago, Mitchell recruited Tyrone to work with him. Tawana soon learned her brother was involved with Mitchell running drugs, putting a rift between them.

I decided not to call Annie until the morning when she would be closer to the Island. I texted her though, urging her to drive carefully and call me when she got on the Island. I also offered her a place to stay.

She called me at eight-forty. "Hey, Annie. You OK? Where are you?"

"I think I'm OK. The five-hour drive gave me time to calm down, but I still can't get over losing both my parents in just over a month. And both murdered. What the fuck is going on?"

"Where are you?"

"Around the corner from you, at the Sheriff's office. But they took my dad to the Coroner's Office in Port Royal. You up for a ride?"

"Sure. Drive over here and park. I'll meet you in front and I'll drive."

"I'll be there in a minute. Thanks, Laz."

Port Royal was an hour away. Hilton Head did not have a coroner, so Beaufort County Coroner's Office served the entire County. It was a pain in the ass drive, but what else could I do for Annie?

By the time I got dressed and out the door, Annie was parking. I jumped out of my car, hugged Annie, and said, "I'm so sorry you're going through this."

We got in my car and headed north. I last made this trip a week ago when I went up to Sullivan's Island, even though Port Royal was only half as far. I wondered whether I had ignited the fire that led to this. I reminded myself that I am an author, not a Private Investigator. Oh yeah, and a murderer.

"Are you going to identify your father?"

"No. My Grammy and Gramps are on their way, or there already."

I knew Annie's Grammy and Gramps were Mitchell's mother and father, but I wasn't certain Annie was in touch with her since her mom's funeral.

"What did the police tell you?"

"Only that a kitchen worker at the diner found him by his car at about eleven last night. I didn't know he was working at the Hilton Head Diner. They said he went off shift at ten o'clock. He parked in the back near the trash dumpster. The diner was not very crowded. The police took statements from the staff and customers that were still there, but no one saw anything. They told me they might know more at the coroner's office. So tell me what you've learned."

"I learned your dad had a small boat and he and Tyrone took it up to Sullivan's Island to pick up drugs. They were selling the shit to the rich kids hanging out down at Coligny Beach. I placed a tracker on the boat and when I saw it heading north one night, I drove to Sullivan's Island.

"I got pictures of four boats and nine people, including your dad and Tyrone. One boat was bigger and seemed to be the supplier. There were three people on that boat.

"I then showed the pictures around to some sources and learned that two on the lead boat were a Hilton Head Town Councilwoman by the name of White, and a Beaufort County Sheriff's Officer, a guy by the name of Baxter."

"Juanita White? I think my mom knew her."

"Yeah. I am speculating, Annie, that someone I talked to may have dimed me out to White or Baxter. If so, they are probably looking for me, but in the meantime, they might assume that your mom's murder investigation led me to your dad and Tyrone. If I am right, that may mean your dad murdered your mom.

"But then again, I think your dad had plenty of enemies and, any of them could have killed him for other reasons."

"If they are looking for you, what are you going to do?"

"I do not think any of my sources know my full name, except for one bartender, and she'd never give me up. If I go back to Philly, the local cops might suspect me for this one and your mom's. And it's frigging cold up in Philly. But I should take you up on that offer to talk to someone at the State Police. I got to get out of the line of fire, and I don't know who to trust locally."

"I'll do it later today. And I'm taking you up on your offer of a bed. I promise to be neat."

"It's a deal."

When we passed the cut-off to Parris Island, I knew we were close. I took Richmond Road down to Old

Shell Road and there it was; the Beaufort County Coroner's Office, a non-descript, one-story red brick building. We parked and Mr. and Mrs. Mitchell were sitting in the lobby, no doubt waiting for Annie. I had never met them.

They stood and embraced Annie. They said nothing. After a minute, they backed off and Annie introduced me. I expressed my deep sorrow for their loss.

Annie asked, "Have you seen your son?"

Mrs. Mitchell nodded.

"I want to see him."

Mrs. Mitchell approached the receptionist and returned, saying, "Give them a minute, Annie, and she'll take you back."

I asked, "You want me to go with you, Annie?"

"No, I'm good, thanks."

They took them to a small conference room off the lobby and they escorted Annie towards the rear of the building.

"It's a shame for that girl, losing her mom and dad so close together. It's not right," Mrs. Mitchell said.

Did she expect me to reply? I better. There's a pregnant pause hanging out there.

"It is a shame, but Annie will be OK. It's terrible for a parent to lose a child also, Mrs. Mitchell."

"I always feared things might end badly for Anton. The boy always had a wild streak in him. You know anything about his death, Mr. Frank?"

"No more than you do," I lied. Let her hear about her son from the police.

Thank goodness Annie joined us, still dabbling at her tears with a tissue.

Annie asked, "What's next?"

Mr. Mitchell replied, "I spoke with Edmund Keith at the funeral home on my way here. He said they would pick up Anton when they heard from the coroner, which he thought would be this afternoon. I'll call Reverend Ayers at Mount Calvary and discuss a funeral. What else is there to do?"

"That should do it," I offered. Obviously, call friends and family. Do you have anyone who can do that for you? That would be very difficult for y'all to do."

"I spoke with my brother earlier. He said he would do it. Can we get out of here?" Mrs. Mitchell asked.

I stood and said, "You should check at the desk, but otherwise I would think we can go."

As we left, Mrs. Mitchell hugged me and said, "Thank you for bringing Annie, Mr. Frank. I hope you can come to the funeral."

"I'll be there, Mrs. Mitchell, and let me know if there's anything I can do in the meantime."

We took off for Hilton Head. After ten minutes of silence, Annie said, "It's weird, Laz. My dad and I had no relationship, and I didn't even like him, but he was my dad, and now it makes me sad to think we never will have a relationship."

"It's not weird, Annie. We only have two parents and now you've lost both. Your feelings are quite normal. Your dad lived the life he did, and it wasn't your fault. If you are up to it, it would be nice if you could go to the funeral home with your Grammy and Gramps. This is very tough on them."

"I'll call them later, thanks."

We spoke little the rest of the way home. Annie was lost in her thoughts, and I allowed her to do so.

I needed to go for a walk, so after getting her settled, giving her the WIFI password, and showing her what was in the fridge, I left her alone.

Chapter 40

When Vernon Brown got back to the precinct, his partner Rumson said, "Captain is waiting for us."

They stood outside her door until she was off the phone and entered after knocking.

"How was the pork sandwich, Vern?"

"Can't a man have any secrets?"

"Who paid?"

"Our CI fund."

"Great. What did Bishop have to say?"

"He'd refer it to DHS and ICE and let them track the bodies. Since the prostitution is related, he thought they would handle that also, at least for the time being."

"Does he know we will continue to pursue O'Connor's murderer? Aren't the Serbs potential suspects? And perhaps the other girls?"

"He knows all of that, but he says if we approach any of them, the trafficking and prostitution case will disappear with the Serbs. In the short term, it leaves me with only the neighborhood bangers, or of course, Hilton Head."

"Vernon, will you forget about Hilton Head? Keep working the neighborhood. Have the unis talk to informants and street kids. Offer a free pass for any leads they can give you. And the current and former employees. Talk to them again, starting with current, and the more recent exes. Leave the thirty years ago peeps like Hilton Head to the last. Where are you with Lena Jovic?"

"Robbie, what do you think about Jovic?"

"I could still be gullible, but I believed her story. She just did not appear a murderer to me. Her blackmail scheme would suggest she's not some wet-behind-the-ears immigrant, but murder is still a gigantic leap."

"I agree with Robbie, Cap. We'll talk to her again, but she's not at the top of my list."

"Other than Mr. Hilton Head, who else is on that list?"

"I'll send you a copy."

"OK, go catch some bad guys."

"You got a list?"

"Not yet, but I will in ten minutes. Lena mentioned she thought O'Connor had a new girlfriend. And we need to find out if there are other kept women at The Logan."

Chapter 41

Two days after being briefed by FBI Special Agent Charles Bishop, ICE sent two investigators from the Enforcement and Removal Operations Team to speak with Lena Jovic. Agent Brian Murphy was the senior investigator, but wanting a female agent with him, he brought Sarah Brookins.

They entered The Locust building at nine-fifty and the uniformed doorman, Christopher Mulligan, greeted them.

Showing their IDs, Murphy said, "Good morning, Mr. Mulligan. We are here to see Ms. Lena Jovic in 1107."

"I'll ring her." After thirty seconds, he hung up his phone. "There does not seem to be an answer. It would seem she is not home."

"Do you have a key?"

"I do not, but I'll call security for you." "Hello, Rachel? Chris Mulligan at the front desk. I have two officers here from ICE wanting access to 1107. I do not know if they have a warrant. Please come over and speak with them."

Five minutes later, an overweight black woman wearing a Globe Securities uniform exited the elevator and approached Murphy and Brookins. "Good morning, officers. I'm Rachel Stokes. How can I help you?"

Showing their badges and handing Stokes the warrant, "As Mr. Mulligan mentioned, we need access to 1107."

Stokes wanted to impress upon them she had some authority, so she took a minute to review the warrant. "Everything looks in order; let's go."

She knocked and waited. And knocked again. Then she opened the door saying; I need to remain with you. I hope that's not a problem."

"None. Just wait here until we clear the place." They took out their their guns and went from room to room, yelling "clear" as they went.

Returning to the entrance, "Murphy said, "It appears she's not here, so you may come in. I can't tell if she's out at the moment or has left for a longer period. There is still some clothing and bedding, but I did not see any jewelry or toiletries. That's unusual in a woman's apartment. Are you aware of any travel plans Ms. Jovic had?"

"I am not, but I'll check and see if there is a note back downstairs. Sometimes residents make us aware of vacation plans so we can check on their units. And Mr. Mulligan might know something."

"We want to do a more thorough search here for mail, messages, phones, or anything that might help us. You're welcome to stay, but we could be another hour. Sarah, you know the drill, bedding, drawers, behind pictures, toilet, and closets. I'll start here. Ms. Stokes, would you call Mr. Mulligan for us, please?"

An hour and twenty minutes later, they had nothing from their search except for some grass and a half dozen unmarked pills.

"I think we are good for today, Ms. Stokes. We may want to send over a forensics team. We will contact the owners of the unit. Thank you for your time."

They walked out together, and Stokes locked up behind them. They took the elevator back to the lobby and thanked her and Chris Mulligan again.

Chapter 42

The Locust was busy today.

At ten after two, Detectives Brown and Rumson walked into the lobby of the condominium building.

In reviewing the units still owned by the Commonwealth REIT, Robbie saw that Lillian Pavlov moved into Unit 1212 six months ago. Recalling that Lena Jovic mentioned her suspicion that O'Connor had a new girlfriend, they decided it was worth talking to her.

Entering the lobby, they encountered Christopher Mulligan, the ever-present doorman.

Showing badges, Brown said, "Good afternoon, Mr. Mulligan. It's us again. Today, we are here to see Ms. Pavlov in Unit 1212."

"Oh my. This is a busy day for law enforcement here at The Locust."

"What do you mean?"

"This morning, two officials from ICE were here looking for Ms. Jovic, the woman you visited last week."

"Oh! How did that go?"

"I don't know. She was not in, but they had a warrant, and Rachel Stokes, in security, let them into her unit. They were there for almost two hours. I'll see if Ms. Pavlov is in."

Brown and Rumson took the elevator to the twelfth floor. Lillian Pavlov opened the door and allowed them in.

"Good afternoon, Ms. Pavlov. Detectives Rumson and Brown. We'd like to ask you a few questions," Ronnie said.

"What kinds of questions?"

"Perhaps we could sit down?"

"Sure. Come in."

Once again, Brown and Rumson found themselves talking to an attractive woman. This one had long, blond hair and appeared to be in her mid-twenties. The apartment was well-furnished and decorated, but they again noticed the lack of any personal pictures or knick-knacks.

"A lovely apartment. Have you been here long?" Rumson asked, already knowing the answer.

"Thank you. I moved in over the summer."

"Where were you living previously?"

"I had an apartment with several other women."

"Where was that?"

"Somewhere in the city. I'm not certain of the address."

"I would think this apartment is quite expensive. What kind of work do you do?"

"I do some modeling."

"May I ask who is paying your rent?"

"What do you mean?"

"We know you did not buy this condo, nor are you paying rent to the owner. So, who is paying your rent, Lilly?"

"My boyfriend owns the place, I think. I don't know. You're right, I'm not paying for it."

"That wasn't difficult, was it? Now, who is your boyfriend?"

"That's rather personal."

Looking at Brown, Rumson said, "Do you think we should take her into the precinct for questioning? She's not very forthcoming here."

"OK. I'll answer. His name is Sean O'Connor."

"And who is paying now that he is deceased?"

"His father is the one who died. Not Sean."

"Your boyfriend is Sean O'Connor, Jr.?" Glancing again at Brown.

"Yes."

"Did you ever meet his father?"

"Yes, I had several dates with him two or three years ago, before I started dating Sean."

"How long have you been in this country, Lilly?"

"Almost four years now."

"Can we see your green card, please?"

Pavlov dug into her purse and handed them her phony green card.

"Do you know Lena Jovic?"

"I only know her name. I think she used to be Sean's father's girlfriend."

"You did not know she lived in this building?"

"No."

"Do you know any other women living in this building?"

"No. It is a very quiet building. A lot of old people here with their little dogs always screeching. I dislike it here. I do not have any friends."

"Do you have any idea who may have killed Sean's father?"

"No, but I can think of many women who may have wanted to. He was a pig."

"When do you expect to see Sean again?"

"I never know. Sometimes he texts me, other times he just comes here. I am expected to be available."

"Vern, any further questions?"

"Let me see your phone, Lilly."

She again reached into her purse and handed Brown her phone.

"I can only call a few people, and only they can call me."

Brown reviewed the phone and saw only four numbers, which were identified as *Sean, Alek, Jelena, and Goric*.

He handed the phone back to her. "Lilly, you should know this green card of yours is fake and you may hear from immigration. We do not think you murdered Sean's father, and that is our only involvement. But others are looking into the people who brought you to this country and made you work the streets. These are crimes and immigration is already looking for Lena Jovic.

"We have all we need for now. We appreciate your time."

They rose and she let them out.

"What do you think, Vern?"

"I think these phone numbers will help ICE track down the Serbs, but I'm not certain we are any closer to finding our murderer."

"How about Junior? Are we going to go talk to him again?"

"I doubt it, Ronnie. I don't think he was involved in his dad's death. He can be ICE's problem. Agree?"

"Yep!"

"But our list of suspects may have increased. Besides current and past employees, all the Serbian girls may have wanted O'Connor dead."

In the lobby, "Thanks again, Chris. I'm sure we'll see you again."

"Goodbye, detectives."

Chapter 43

Two days after the funeral of Anton Mitchell, Annie and I were on our way to the South Carolina Law Enforcement Division (SLED) office in Charleston.

Annie's high school friend, Ryan Goodwin, contacted his father, Major Clifford Goodwin.

Goodwin was the Assistant Director of SLED's Homeland Security Division in the SLED Headquarters in Columbia but agreed to drive to Charleston to meet us.

SLED was like most other State Police offices except South Carolina had a separate division that handled Traffic and Highway Control. When I spoke with Goodwin on the phone, he said most likely their Narcotics, Alcohol, and Vice Services Division would handle it, but he thought I should meet with him first.

I hated the two-hour drive to Charleston, as it always took me almost three, and then finding my destination and parking another twenty minutes. We left at seven-thirty for our eleven o'clock meeting and parked by ten-forty-five. Enough time for a second cup of coffee and a pee for me.

A receptionist escorted us to a small conference room and Clifford Goodwin, in full khaki tan uniform, joined us. They take this military crap pretty seriously, I gathered. I thought about saluting, but stood and shook his hand. "I'm Frank Lazarus. I think you have met Annie Chaplin."

"Good morning. Yes, I have met Annie. How are you, Annie?"

"I'm good, Mr. Goodwin. Thanks for meeting us. How's Ryan?"

"Ryan is doing very well. I'll, of course, tell him we met, if you don't call him first. He's in his fifth year at Clemson, but he promises me this will be his last year. He may go to Law School and the FBI, so I'm not certain if or when he'll get a job.

"So, tell me what you have here. And give me as much detail as you can, please. I hope it's OK if I record this. Saves me taking notes and I'll pass along a more accurate account."

"Fine with me," I said. "I'll start. I dated Annie's mom, Tawana, for nine months, and when I returned from Philadelphia a month ago, the Beaufort County Detectives stopped by and told me someone murdered Tawana. I was their first suspect, but I think I convinced them I spent the night in Florence on my way back.

"I stopped by to see Tawana's mother and Annie came out to tell me I was not welcome by Mrs. Chaplin, but Annie wanted to talk to me after the funeral. We had dinner after that and Annie said Tawana found out that her brother, Tyrone, was doing some business with her ex-husband, and Annie's father, Anton Mitchell. You still with me?"

"I think so. Keep going."

"I wish I could make this story shorter, sorry. I contacted someone I knew and asked about Mitchell. I was told he was a bad dude and suspected to be selling drugs down in the Coligny Beach area. Mitchell had a small boat and took it up to Sullivan's Island to pick up the drugs. I put a tracker on the boat, and one night, I followed it up to Sullivan's Island.

" Over the two hours, I saw four boats in total and nine people; one boat with Mitchell and Tyrone. I took pictures of all nine people. A source of mine identified two of them as Juanita White, a Hilton Head Town Councilwoman, and Alan Baxter of the Beaufort County's Sheriff's Office."

I handed him my phone with the pictures opened.

"Oh shit," was all Goodwin said.

"A couple of days later, someone killed Mitchell. One has to believe this is all related, but I knew I could do no more. I was afraid to take this to the Beaufort County Sheriff's Office, for obvious reasons. I thought of the FBI office in Atlanta, but when Annie said she knew your son, here we are."

"This will get ugly, no doubt. Baxter has been on our radar for a while for nothing more than he advanced too quickly in the Sheriff's Office.

"He has an uncle who retired down in Beaufort County and facilitated promotions and glowing reports. Someone buried several military disciplinary actions."

"You think Annie and me are in danger?"

"I couldn't say. Who knows of your involvement?"

"I fear that someone I spoke with gave me up, perhaps unintentionally. But none of those sources knew my last name. And I do not know who knows that Annie and I have spoken."

"When are you going back to Atlanta, Annie?"

"I was going to drive back on Sunday, but I can leave tomorrow."

"I think that is a good idea. I don't think anyone wants you bad enough to chase you down in Atlanta.

"Frank, I have more concerns about you. I'm not certain there is enough evidence yet to make arrests. I will turn this over to Major Butch Weir in the NAV Division. You have anywhere you can hide out for a while?"

"I don't have anyone I can spend a month with, but I have five or six friends in Florida I may spend two or three nights with. But I might stay low profile right on Hilton Head. There is a bartender I know who may want company. I'll let you know."

"I'll ask Butch Weir to contact you tomorrow and advise who your contact will be. Annie, you get back to Atlanta. I appreciate you both bringing this matter to me. Have a safe trip back to Hilton Head."

We stood, shook hands, and got out of Dodge.

IslandGate was turning dangerous for your favorite author.

Chapter 44

When I awoke the next day, I saw a message from Annie stating that at eleven-forty last night; she was back in Atlanta.

It was time for me to get away. I emailed Donna Ellick in Boca Raton, Florida, telling her my apartment needed some work done, and might I spend a few nights with her during repairs. Donna and I dated briefly fifteen years ago, and she made it into my book, *103 FIRST DATES: MISMATCH DOTCOM*. Since then, I knew she lived with a man who disappeared on her, and more recently, she was dating a guy she claimed, "Was not the one."

At eleven o'clock I got her reply: *CALL ME.*

I did. "Mr. Lazarus, what a pleasant surprise. How the hell are you?"

"I'm good, Donna. Yourself?"

"About the same. I'm going to get to see you?"

"That's up to you. I know it's winter and you may have visitors, but if your guest bedroom is available, you'd do me a huge favor, and it would be great to see you. Hopefully, it would only be for a few days. But I have other options, Donna, so you can be honest. It's been a long time since we've seen each other."

"First, I have no company, so you are welcome. I am still seeing Steve. I think I mentioned him to you. But it would be a great excuse not to see him. I'll tell him I have company from Philly. If I'm lucky, we can stretch this into a couple of months. When are you coming?"

"Google Maps says it's a seven-hour drive, but it will take me at least eight, maybe a bit more. Too late for today, so I'll leave in the morning. I'll be there for dinner."

"If my memory serves me, I owe you a dinner from fifteen years ago. I invited you to dinner, and you came up with some lame excuse."

"I spent seven years making lame excuses, and a few good ones. But don't go to any trouble, Donna. I'll not be up to going out, but pizza or Chinese would be great. And I'll take you to dinner Sunday night."

"Chinese it is; I haven't had it since Christmas. That was a month ago. Let me give you my address. Update me during the drive. I'm looking forward to seeing you, Frank."

"Ditto, and thanks Donna. You're a lifesaver."

You heard the conversation. What do you think are her expectations? What are mine? I have not seen the woman in fifteen years. She could be in a wheelchair knitting with no teeth or hair. Is this a mistake? Arlene Feinberg in Fort Lauderdale was my second choice, but that's an hour further, and I think Arlene has a cat.

Why do I do these things?

I don't know if I am packing for two days or two weeks. But it's Florida. All I need are undies, tee shirts and shorts. I add a bathing suit to the pile, medications, hearing aids, chargers for all my devices, and my toilet kit.

I emailed my concierge to hold any packages. There was no one else I needed to notify, but I sent Annie an email to let her know I was leaving.

Chapter 45

I was in my car the next morning at eight AM with a cup of coffee in hand. I had a forty-five-minute drive to reach I-95, and I'd get a second cup of coffee before I got on 95. It would then take me two hours to drive through Georgia. Traffic would be unpredictable, but at this hour, there was no red on my phone and only a couple of short orange lines. I expected it to get heavier as I progressed south.

I texted Donna that I was on my way. I got a thumbs-up and smiley-face reply.

It was eleven-twenty when I reached the Florida border and stopped for a pee and grapefruit juice break. I updated Donna.

An hour later, I saw my first Wawa sign and stopped for gas, more coffee, and two soft pretzels. It was nice to be back in a civilized state, the governor notwithstanding.

After I resumed my drive, my phone rang. UKNOWN CALLER, per my Caller ID. I answered anyway.

"Hello?"

"Hello, is this Mr. Lazarus?"

"Yes, I'm Frank Lazarus. Who's this?"

"Yes, sir. I'm Officer Chad Winters with the SLED ANV Division up in Columbia. Major Butch Weir asked me to call you and introduce myself. He assigned me to the matter you discussed with him, and we are starting our investigation today.

"I can't tell you how long this might take, but knowing some participants and their boats is a good start. They may change their meeting spot from Sullivan's Island, but we'll get a warrant to put tracking devices on their cars and boats.

"I'm calling on my cell, so you'll have my number. May I suggest you get a burner phone and turn off your phone? Butch told me you are out of town, and we don't want anyone tracking you. If you do, text me the number. Contact me if you need me, and I'll be in touch when we know more."

"I'll do that, and thanks, Chad. Bye."

Where the hell do I buy a burner phone? Amazon, of course, but I need it today. Walmart was my second choice.

At my next pee stop, I discovered the nearest Walmart was in Delray Beach, eight miles before my Boca exit.

It turned out to be a twenty-minute diversion while I bought an AT&T pre-paid Samsung Galaxy cellphone and purchased several decent bottles of Cabernet, and a bottle of Ketel One.

I called Donna. "Where are you?"

"I had to make a quick stop in Delray, but I'm back on 95."

"You're about a half hour away. We have outdoor visitor parking. Give them the car information when you come into the lobby. Any problems, call me. See you soon."

"You got it, Donna."

Thirty-five minutes later, I pulled into the parking lot of One Thousand Ocean Condominiums. Visitor parking was full except for the handicapped parking, and I pulled into it. I still had my handicap tag from my hip surgery ten years ago. I did as I was told in the lobby, and the concierge called up to Donna for clearance.

The building was U-shaped, facing the ocean. It was an older building, but everything looked new and expensively furnished. The security guard gave me a tag for my car, which I put on the mirror, returned, and took the elevator to the fifth floor.

I went to knock on 508 but the door opened, and Donna was there with a big smile and open arms. "Welcome to Boca, Frank Lazarus. You look the same. Come on in."

"You look better if that's possible, Donna. Florida agrees with you. Nice tan in January."

Donna looked great, like she had spent the last two days in a health & beauty spa. She was wearing a white tank top showing both her midriff and very nice cleavage. She had on black Capri pants that came to her mid-calf, and white sandals.

I stepped into her foyer and perused the room. It was huge, with high ceilings, expensive furniture, and a to-die-for ocean view. I knew she had family money, and she had done very well in business..

"What can I get you? Come in and let me show you around."

"Nothing right now, Donna. Before anything, I'd like to get cleaned up. And then a drink while we decide about dinner."

She gave me a quick tour of the master and guest bedrooms, and said, "You can shower here or use the one in the master bath. It has six jet sprays that might knock you on your butt."

"That's tempting, but I'll use the guest shower. I won't be long."

"You still doing your vodka straight on the rocks? And you remembered I drink Cab? Very sweet of you."

"Lucky guess, and yes, to rocks."

She left. I closed the door to the guest suite, unpacked my toilet kit, and jumped in the shower.

Fifteen minutes later, a refreshed me walked out, and she was in the kitchen, having set out our drinks at the counter. She also had a cheese plate and cashews. I handed her the soft pretzels I bought.

"Someone made a Wawa stop, I see."

"At the first one I saw." I sat down on the stool with the vodka in front of it and she sat next to me. We picked up her glasses and asked, "What are we toasting to?"

I suggested, "Friendship?"

She responded, "How about mulligans?"

"To mulligans."

***

We ordered Chinese delivery and had a second drink. Donna told me about Gary, the no-good son-of-a-bitch who jilted her, her daughter and grandkids, her life in Boca, and her current beau, Steve Ivens.

I told her about my kids and grandkids, and my life on Hilton Head. I decided to tell her about Tawana, but not the after-death theatrics, or the real reason I was in Boca.

A young Asian man delivered the food, and we feasted on spare ribs, egg rolls, moo shu, and sweet and sour shrimp. I took the Michelob Ultra she offered me, and she had a third glass of wine.

We wrapped the leftovers, cleaned up the kitchen, and took our drinks to the patio, where there was a nice ocean breeze.

"It's lovely here, Donna. Looks like you have a great life here. You deserve it."

"Thanks, Frank. I can't complain, even though there is a piece missing since Gary's departure."

I raised my glass and said, "Here's to you finding the missing piece."

"Thanks. You want coffee or dessert?"

"No, thanks, Donna." Looking at my watch, I said, "I'm dozing on you. I think I'll turn in, and see if I can read a bit before falling asleep. You have plans tomorrow?"

"I play Maj Jong with some women on Sunday morning, but I can skip it if you want to do something."

"No, that's fine. Play, and if I get up, I can do some writing."

"OK, but I'll want to hear about the book tomorrow."

When I stood, she also stood. "Thank you again for taking me in. I can't tell you how much I appreciate this. And tomorrow night, dinner is on me."

I embraced her and gave her a peck on the cheek. She held on a bit longer than I expected, and I feared she might feel my attraction.

"Good night."
"See you in the morning."
Whew!

Chapter 46

Vernon Brown was in early the next morning, but not before Captain Webster. He stopped at her office to debrief her on their interview with Lilly Pavlov yesterday.

"Morning, Cap. Got a sec?"

"Always, Vern. Good morning to you. No donuts?"

"Sorry. We met with Lilly Pavlov yesterday at the Locust. She was the newest renter of the REITs-owned condos there.

"She is Sean Jr.'s girlfriend, not the old man's. Doesn't help us much, but he's part of whatever is going on there. And guess what? ICE was there earlier looking for Lena Jovic and they believe she has fled to parts unknown.

"They gave Lilly a burner phone, and we got the four phone numbers that include the three Serb overseers. This should help ICE locate them, but if I give it to them, it leaves us out in the cold again. Any of these girls could have killed O'Connor."

"Let's talk this out, Vern. Tell me how any of these girls would have known O'Connor was at a basketball game that night, and if they did, how did they get to St. Joe's with a gun? None of them had cars we know of. Did they take SEPTA? I'm not seeing that, Vern."

"I guess you're right. When Lilly told us how the girls hated him, I added them all to the suspect list. But if any of them were to kill him, they most likely would have done it in bed.

"Next step, Robbie and I are going to the O'Connor office today to re-interview all the current employees. We'll start with the most senior and work our way to the newest employees."

"Are we getting anything out of the neighborhood CIs or anyone out there?"

"Crickets, Cap."

"I'll talk to McCarthy later, see if he can bring some heat. Keep me posted, Vern. We have to be getting closer."

"You think so? I'm not so certain. Have a good one."

When he returned to his desk, Robbie was on the phone. When she hung up, "I just spoke with Beverly Sample, O'Connor's Operations Vice President, and she'll have a couple of offices for us and alert the employees. Five of them are working remotely today."

"The Cap says we might as well give the Serb phone numbers to ICE. It's unlikely any of those girls did the murder. Let's go."

Thirty-five minutes later, they walked into the World Headquarters of The O'Connor Group and asked for Beverly Sample. She arrived promptly and said, "Good morning, detectives. Let's go to Mr. O'Connor's office and discuss your plans for the day."

She led them to the rear of the large office suite to O'Connor senior's office. "Would you care for coffee?"

"If it's easy, I'll take black."

"Ditto," Rumson said.

She called someone and asked for three coffees, all black.

"This office is available, as is Sean Jr's, as he is not in today. Do you want to meet with everyone? In any order?"

"Yes, everyone who is here today. As best you can, we would like to start with the most senior employees and work our way up. We can start with you since you're here."

"That's fine but let me get my assistant organizing this. When you finish with one employee, they can let Jean know, and she'll have the next one come in." She made the call.

"OK! Fire away."

"How long have you been here, Beverly?"

"It will be twelve years in March."

"Where did you work previously?"

"I worked for Simpson, Kroll, and Gallager, LLC, in Cherry Hill. When O'Connor acquired the firm, they offered me this position."

"We have heard this is a tough place to work, employee turnover is high, and the O'Connors are tough bosses."

"I would say that all the above are true. But I also think with the senior's demise, things could improve. He could be quite impulsive, and he refused to adhere to any protocols we put in place for employee performance reviews or discipline. It made my job difficult."

"Are you aware of any romantic entanglements either of the O'Connors may have had with employees?"

"Oh, boy. When I first got here, there was a pending lawsuit against Mr. O'Connor. I did not get involved with it and I understood they settled soon after. Two years ago, at her exit interview, Dawn Jordan said that Sean Jr. was harassing her to go out with him. It was the reason she left. I cannot tell you there are no other incidents, but these are the only ones I am aware of."

"Are there any women working here of Serbian descent?"

"Wow. Where's that question coming from? None that I am aware of, but Helen Wargo has a slight accent that could be Eastern European. I'm not very good at identifying accents other than New York and Mississippi."

"Thank you, Beverly. This is quite helpful. Robbie, why don't you stay here, and I'll go to the other office."

"Our most senior employee by twenty-five years is our VP of Technology Systems, James Talarico."

"Who wants to start with him?"

Brown said, "I'll take him."

He stood and left with Sample. She stopped at her assistant's desk and then she got me settled in Sean Jr's office.

Shortly thereafter, there was a knock at the door, and I yelled, *ENTER!*

James Talarico entered, and we shook hands. He was about six feet tall, with salt and pepper hair and a full beard. He dressed in jeans and a 76ers sweatshirt. He carried a pen and pad of paper, thinking I might ask him to research something.

"Good morning, Mr. Talarico. Please have a seat. I know we interviewed you after Mr. O'Connor's death, but we are re-interviewing everyone. We started with the most senior employees, and you have that honor by about twenty-five years, it appears."

"I think you are right about that. It doesn't seem like forty years, but I can't hide from it either."

"How have you managed that?"

"It could be I'm lazy and remaining in my comfort zone. But I like to think that I have stayed below the radar and have become indispensable over the years. I avoid the surrounding chaos. The O'Connors know very little about technology and leave me on my own. It works, and I like Beverly a lot."

"Some might say *you know where the bodies are buried*."

"Perhaps figuratively, but I can assure you, not literally."

"Can you think of any ex-employees who left here upset or who made threats?"

"Not enough to commit murder, but several left here less than quietly. None stick out to me though as particularly threatening. I do not know your business, sir, but I would think that the more recent terminations would be more likely threats than those who may have left ten or twenty years ago. Beverly could tell you more."

"Did you, or do you, remain in contact with any former employees?

"A few, but only for a year or two, and then their curiosity about what is going on here fades. But now that you're asking, a year or so ago, I got a call out of the blue from a real old-timer, Frank Lazarus. We got together for dinner and caught up."

"He's the guy from Hilton Head?"

"Yeah."

"Did he want to know anything specific?"

"We caught up on our families, the Eagles, Sixers, and he asked about old man O'Connor."

"What did he want to know about him?"

"Not much. Was he still working and did he come into the office? Stuff like that."

"What do you know about his termination?"

"It was a long time ago, but I would guess it was about money. But Frank was a great guy, and I know his sales team went with him. They did very well for themselves with MassMutual."

"Have you heard from him since?"

"Yeah, a sympathy emoji when the Sixers got knocked out of the playoffs again."

"I think that's it for now, James. I appreciate your time. Would you ask Jean to send the next person in? Thanks."

Hilton Head again, Brown thought to himself.

Chapter 47

Two days later, all the employees had been re-interviewed, including those who were working remotely.

Only one new name surfaced, Dawn Jordan, who resigned and alleged sexual harassment from Sean Jr.

"Hey Vern; am I allowed to call you an idiot?"

"You would not be the first, Robbie, nor the last. What did I do this time?"

"It's both of us." She walked over to his desk and put a piece of paper in front of him.

"You recall the REIT retained ownership of twelve units at The Locust? Only eight are occupied, and look at the list of names:

Lena Jovic
Lillian Pavlov
Hai Fu Wang
Fen Huang
Clara Bengtsson
Ingrid Ecklund
Mahalia Williams

Jamika Anderson

"Anything strike you?"

"All women, single women, no doubt, and they are not all Serbian?"

"Right, boss. We thought this was an isolated trafficking cell, but it seems much more."

"Very interesting, Robbie, but it doesn't help us. We've convinced ourselves that none of these girls could have killed O'Connor, so it's more fodder for ICE."

"I'll send it over to them."

"You want to run down that Dawn Jordan while I stay working the ex-employee list?"

"Will do."

***

After getting the Serbs' phone numbers from the Philly PD, ICE Agent Brian Murphy asked Michele Brodsky to put together a map showing the locations of the phones for more than an hour, the time of day, and the duration of the stay at that location.

He hoped they could spot a pattern that would show where the girls were being kept, and/or their base of operations.

By three in the afternoon, Brodsky sat down with Murphy and Sarah Brookins.

"First, I got nothing at all on the Vulic phone. You recall he's the guy who worked in Belgrave and may not even come to this country. And there were no calls from Jovic's phone to his.

"But I think the Dacic woman gives us what we need. She never leaves the block between Susquehanna, Broad, Dauphin, and Park Streets. That's a residential and small store area, beauty salons, pizza shops, and the like. It's just north of the Temple Campus.

"Loncar spends time there, but he's all over town, hotels, Chinatown, and Old City. And he has many stops from thirty to forty-five minutes."

Murphy interjected, "That makes sense. Loncar is the pimp and most likely staking out the girls' locations. The key, as you pointed out, is Dacic. She's the girls' overseer and lives with them. But we do not have the exact location, so I am hesitant raiding some unknown building."

Brodsky said, "Why not let me go down there and snoop around? I'll see if I can identify a building and the comings and goings of the occupants. It would give me a chance to do some fieldwork."

"Why don't the two of you go down there? You can try during the afternoon, but you may need to go back at night when there is more activity. Dress in jeans and sweatshirts. Do nothing to attract attention and be discreet when taking pictures. You have a zoom lens?"

"I do. We can do this. We'll go down tomorrow at about three, and then we can stay into the evening."

"Sounds good, thanks, Shelley, and you too, Sarah."

Sarah suggested she drive, as her VW Beetle would be easier to park than Shelley's SUV, and she would be free to scope out the area. When they arrived, they drove around the area twice, noting the buildings in the neighborhood.

Broad Street was mostly commercial buildings, but on the east side, across from the legendary Uptown Theater, the buildings were three and four stories, with retail on the ground floor and apartments above them.

The other three streets on the block were residential or vacant lots, except for a barbecue chicken place on Susquehanna Street. They agreed it had to be one of the buildings on Broad Street. The busyness of a major artery, combined with the stop for The Broad Street Subway line, would protect the anonymity of the hideaway.

They parked in the middle of the block in front of the Uptown. They could see up and down the block from there. Before settling in, they walked down to the market they passed for coffee and snacks to sustain them. They made mental notes of the buildings that might serve a group of twenty to forty young women. Several appeared large enough, but there was no traffic in or out.

Once they settled, Sarah looked up the street and Shelley down.

The two women got to know each other since they had never worked together. They were both single, but from very different backgrounds. Sarah was from Southwest Philadelphia and went to Temple University for Criminal Justice. Shelley was from Devon on the Main Line and had a law degree from Villanova.

To kill time and learn each other's secrets, they played *Two Truths and A Lie*. Shelley learned Sarah still favored Motown music like her pop-pop, and Sarah learned Shelley gave up her virginity at seventeen in a storeroom at Conestoga High School.

Sarah had nothing to report on north-end pedestrian traffic, but Shelley saw two well-dressed men exit one building, and two other men enter.

At six-fifteen, one young woman dressed in a miniskirt and fake fur jacket exited the same building and jumped into a waiting car. They got pictures of the woman and the two men exiting.

Pedestrian traffic increased significantly with people getting on and off buses and coming and going from the subway entrance.

The only building that had more than two people enter was the same target building. The address was 2233 North Broad Street and had a small awning that said *UPTOWN APARTMENTS*.

At eight o'clock, they decided they had enough, and the UPTOWN APARTMENTS was the place. It had three stories and a basement. There was no retail store on the ground floor, they had four floors of living space. And the house was deep; they estimated it to be between seventy and eighty feet.

"Let's get out of this neighborhood and grab something to eat," Sarah suggested. "Is your car back at the office?"

"Yeah, but you got to decide where to eat."

"Sabrina's it is; it's on the way and I rarely get to go there."

"Sounds good."

Chapter 48

The next morning I awoke at my usual seven AM, but the condo was quiet and not wanting to wake Donna, I did my stretching, read, checked all my email, looked at the headlines on Huffington Post and ESPN, and then played WORDLE and Connections.

By eight-thirty, I smelled coffee and went out to the kitchen. She was sitting at the counter with coffee and a bagel, and I said, "Good morning."

"Hey, sleepyhead. Good morning to you. Did you sleep OK?"

"I slept great, but I've been up for a while. The bed is very comfortable, and the place is quiet. What time is Maj Jong?"

"Nine down in our Community Room. You want some breakfast?"

"I'll make some coffee and perhaps have one of those. I'll raid your fridge or perhaps run out and pick up some eggs or something. You need anything from the store?"

"I don't think so. If you go out, back two blocks is a Publix, and across the street is a Wawa. You can't go wrong."

"I may see a sausage Sizzli in my future."

"Looks like a nice day for the beach or pool. So tell me about the book you're writing."

"The short version, it's about this."

"This what?"

"Just this. It's about the last year of my life. Some of it is complete fiction, then some, like my visiting you, are real life. The reader will have to decide which is which. And characters from my prior books make cameo appearances. Detective Vernon Brown is in it, of course, and some others. I'm having fun writing it. I can explore my dark side, and everyone can think it is fiction."

"Hmmm, I may need to see what you write about this stop in Boca. I'll do my best to make it an exciting chapter. OK, I'm off. I'll see you around noon. Here's a key and a fob to get into the building."

"I'll be fine. Have fun."

I wrote for an hour and then sat on the patio reading with a second cup of coffee. Then another hour of writing.

You might call it snooping, but I took a tour of the house again, this time on my own. I wanted to see that shower. What is it about medicine cabinets that people cannot pass them by?

I peeked in and saw the usual medications: aspirin, Advil, Tylenol, Xanax, and Sertraline, along with Q-tips, Band-Aids, etc. Oh yeah, a pouch with a white powder. If I'm not mistaken, it was cocaine. Great! What do I do with this information?

Donna returned at noon, as promised.

"Hey, how much did you win?"

"I wish. I lost $7.50. A tough day at the table. What did you do?"

"I never made it out. I wrote and sat out on your patio for a while. Do you have neighbors who smoke weed?"

"I think the old couple downstairs does; they say it helps them sleep. Do you do it?"

"Me? Never. I'm sure if I lit up, I would do a Richard Pryor and blow myself up."

"I think that was crack, Frank."

"It involved a flame, didn't it?"

We had a quick lunch and sat at the pool for two hours. I went for a walk on the beach. When I returned, Donna was in her bedroom, so I showered and read some more.

Like Hilton Head, the Early Bird Specials for dinner started at four o'clock, and by seven, everyone was home. We bucked that trend and had a six o'clock reservation at the Boca Raton Beach Club, a short walk from Donna's.

We, of course, convened for drinks at five. Donna wore a bright orange top with one-shoulder bare, white capris, white sandals, and orange and gold jewelry.

I wore white shorts and a long-sleeve blue dress shirt with the tails out; my dressy casual look.

This is my book, so I will not bore you with the details of our dinner conversation and what we ate. If you must know, I had linguini and clams.

We stopped for ice cream on the walk back and were back at the condo by eight-fifteen.

"You up for another glass of wine?" she asked.

"Sure, I can't let you drink alone."

She brought two half-filled glasses of red wine, handed me mine, and sat next to me on the couch.

"Are we still toasting to find the missing pieces?" she asked.

"Sure."

We clinked glasses and took sips of our wine. We placed our glasses on the coffee table. She then rolled over onto me and straddled my lap. "You've been here twenty-fours now, Frank. How long do you think I am going to wait for you to make a move?"

"I can assure you, you would not have waited much longer."

With that, we kissed and continued doing so while she unbuttoned my shirt, and I pondered how I was going to undress her. I didn't have to wait long as she stood, pulled me up, and led me to her bedroom.

This overture was premeditated, as she had lit candles and turned down the bed.

We made love slowly and passionately, at least as slowly as I could, which was not very slow.

We fell asleep in each other's arms.

Chapter 49

When I woke at seven-fifteen, I went to the guest bathroom, brushed my teeth, and returned to bed. As I got comfy, she opened one eye, smiled, and said, "Are you up for good?"

"I'm not sure."

She then flipped the sheets back, went down, and took me in her mouth. I returned the favor, tasting her. But sensing my approaching explosion, she climbed on top of me, inserting Mr. Johnson into her. She remained there for another minute or two and then collapsed next to me. We stayed interlocked for twenty minutes with little being said.

Then I said, "Do I get to use the master shower now?"

"You want company?"

"I'd love company."

We showered with all six of the jet sprays on. We washed each other's privates and continued canoodling.

After dressing, we went out to breakfast. Donna had some errands to run, and I told her I was fine writing and reading. I could not resist checking the medicine cabinet again and found the pouch of blow gone. I understood more about her errands this morning.

I took the opportunity to call Arlene Feinberg in Fort Lauderdale.

"Hello?" she answered.

"Arlene, don't be shocked, but it's Frank Lazarus calling from Hilton Head. Happy New Year. How are you?"

"I am shocked, Frank. Happy New Year to you too. Things are good with me. Is something up? I mean, when was the last time we spoke?"

"Yes, something is up. They need to do some work in my apartment, and it may take a few days. I thought I might head south to get some beach time in Florida. I thought of you first. If you could stand me for a few days, I'd appreciate it, but I have other options, so please do not feel any pressure."

"That would be great, Frank. Let me think about what I have going on here. No visitors, for sure. I have lunch plans tomorrow with a couple of girlfriends. On Wednesday, I am meeting a client in the morning to discuss decorating a couple of rooms. But other than that, I'm good. When are you thinking?"

"First, whatever you need to do, Arlene, do it. I don't need babysitting or tour guiding. I can do some writing, reading, walking, whatever.

"I thought I'd leave early tomorrow morning. It's an eight or nine-hour drive, so that should get me there late afternoon. And please do not go to any trouble. We can eat out."

"How long might you want to stay?"

"Two, three nights at the most."

"Great. Did I ever tell you my cat died, and I did not replace it?"

"Oh, I'm so sorry, Arlene," I lied for about the tenth time in this conversation. "I'll text you in the morning when I get on the road. And thanks again, Arlene. It will be great to see you."

"Looking forward to it. Bye, Frank."

I owe you an explanation. Donna is great, attractive, sexy, funny, and passionate. But I'm never going to be with a weed and cocaine user, so it's best I cut it short now before she thinks I am *that missing piece* for her.

If you're wondering, Arlene and I have never been a couple. We had one make-out session twenty years ago after a high school reunion. The cats were always a deal-breaker for me, but I never told her that.

Donna got home at eleven-twenty, loaded down with packages. I ran to take one from her and said, "You had a busy morning. Whatta you got here?"

"I'm making that dinner I promised you fifteen years ago-Roasted chicken, mashed potatoes, asparagus almondine, and a Caesar Salad. Sound OK?"

"Sounds fabulous, but I told you not to go to any trouble."

"Will you stop that, please? It's no trouble. I love to cook but don't do it much for myself. What did you do all morning?"

"I have some good news and some bad news. I got a call; my apartment is ready."

"Oh, is that the good or the bad?"

"Yes!"

"And I was getting used to having you here. Let's not waste time."

She came over to me and hugged me while kissing and underdressing me at the same time.

Cocktails, dinner, and final night goodbye sex were great.

In the morning, I showered and finished packing while she slept. I had to leave by eight so she would think I was going back to Hilton Head. She was up and dressed and waiting in the kitchen. We had coffee.

She put her arms around my neck and said, "What happens now?"

"You mean today?"

"No, I mean for you and me."

"I don't know, Donna. Hopefully, you might come to visit me, or I can get back down here. It has been great spending time with you. But Steve is in your life, and

I don't want to complicate that. But I hope this is not the end for us."

"Frank, you've always been full of shit. I'll worry about Steve, and I will visit you, just tell me when. I am more convinced than ever that we are good together. Have a safe trip and let me know when you're home safe and sound."

"Will do, Donna, and thank you again for everything."

I walked out the door thinking that we might be good together, if...

But for now, I need to get focused on Arlene.

Chapter 50

Major Butch Weir asked Major Goodwin to join him in a meeting with Chad Winters and his partner, Cookie Flores.

"Chad, bring us to date on the status of Frank Lazarus and Annie Chaplin."

"Sure. I spoke this morning with Lazarus, who took our advice and was on his way to Florida. I think we all believe he might be in the greatest danger. Annie Chaplin returned to her home in Atlanta two days ago. She has returned to work. I'll check in again with her in a day or two."

Goodwin added, "I called Annie this morning, Chad, and she seems fine. She admits to being paranoid and has asked a male friend to stay at her place overnight. She's also worried about Lazarus."

"What's the relationship with her and Lazarus?" Weir wanted to know.

"They only met three times before someone killed her mother. Since then, they have gotten close. Annie grew up on the Island and still returns when she can."

Weir said, "So, other than the runners, we have Baxter and White, as the leaders of this ring. What else do we know about this outfit?"

Flores said, "I can take this one, Chad. We know more about the locations than about all the participants, Chief.

"Even though Baxter and White are both in Beaufort County, we believe Charleston is the hub and supplies the coastal areas from Jacksonville, Florida up to Wilmington, North Carolina, with contact points in Myrtle Beach, Pawley's Island, Edisto, Beaufort, Hilton Head and Tybee.

"We're speculating there is another stop or two between Tybee and Jacksonville, most likely St. Simons or Amelia."

Chad added, "We've got no other names, but suspect others like White are involved at local levels. We believe Baxter is running the show. And, they seem to work the tourists. Further inland, there are other suppliers to locals and permanent residents of the area."

Weir said, "Taking this in steps, I think I need to call the Beaufort County Chairman and Hilton Head's mayor to give them a heads-up on what's coming. We'll get a warrant to put a tracker on Baxter's boat and look into his financials.

"Then, Chad, you and I will visit Juanita White and perhaps make a deal with her. Any other thoughts or suggestions?"

Goodwin said, "I think this needs to be kept on a fast track. It might be tough to keep the lid on this for very long."

"I agree, Cliff. I'll make the calls today, and we'll try to meet with White in the next two days. Chad, why don't you call her?"

The meeting was over, and the wheels of justice were in motion.

Chapter 51

The next morning, Michele Brodsky and Sarah Brookins met with Brian Murphy to discuss their surveillance yesterday, and their next step.

"We are certain this address, 2233 North Broad Street, is their base, Brian," said Brookins.

"Any idea how many people are in there, and the security?"

"There was no visible security in the front or back, except for cameras. We saw seven girls coming or going, and four Johns. But this is a large, four-story building, and I would speculate they have one or two floors set up with suites to host visitors, then dorm-like facilities for the girls, and another floor for offices, kitchen, dining, and whatever. There could be thirty to forty girls in there."

"We have enough to raid the place and make arrests for prostitution and trafficking, but we would only get the small fish. To nail O'Connor and/or Kapustin, we need to review that money trail again. What do we have there?"

Brookins answered, "I think we are good there, Brian. We have O'Connor's account at ELK and other O'Connor-controlled businesses funding the ELKSPO account in the Caymans, and that account is paying rent to the Commonwealth REIT for the girls' apartments. O'Connor and Kapustin are all over these accounts.

"That account is also making payments to Aleksander Vulic, Jelena Dacic, and Goric Loncar, as well as yet unidentified individuals. Kapustin may claim he was only *paying the bills*, but the court will see right through that."

Murphy added, "But with the latest names we received from the Philly PD, we know there is more than just this Serbian cluster involved. I think once we start peeling this onion, we are going to find several layers of wrongdoing. But we need to start and hope that A will lead us to B and C. They'll all be begging us to make deals. Let's go."

"We will schedule the arrests of Kapustins, father and son, Feldman, and O'Connor to coincide with the raid on Broad Street. We'll need three teams, the largest one going to Broad Street.

"We'll need a bus or large van to collect the girls. We are going to need to house them somewhere until we can interview them all, and then decide if to jail, deport, or grant them asylum. A higher pay grade will make that call. We good?"

"We're good. Can we keep Shelley here on our team? She's been great."

"Shelley, do you want to ask your boss if you can stick with us to see this campaign through?"

"Love to. Thanks for the opportunity."

Murphy ended the meeting by saying, "Let's target everything two days from now, the 28th."

Chapter 52

I had the entire day from eight until four to kill while Donna thought I was driving to Hilton Head, and Arlene thought I was driving from Hilton Head to Fort Lauderdale. My drive from Boca to Lauderdale only took a half hour, and I had breakfast at the Floridian on Las Olas Boulevard.

I then went to Las Olas Promenade Park and sat on a bench overlooking the Inter-Coastal Waterway and read for two hours. I walked an hour up to the Ritz-Carlton Hotel and had a Cobb Salad for lunch at the outdoor cafe, then took a nap in the lobby. I amaze myself on how I can waste time with great efficiency.

One more stop at Trader Joe's for more wine and flowers, and, at ten before four, I was looking for Arlene's. She lived on NW 4th Court in what you might call a cottage or bungalow. I could tell this was her place, as I knew she was a gardener, and her house stood out in a mixed neighborhood of well-kept homes, with some less-well-kept ones scattered in.

I pulled into her driveway; her Rav4 was under the carport. She must have been looking out the window as she stepped outside before I could retrieve my bag.

"I cannot believe you are here," as she threw her arms around me and kissed me. No need to wonder what was on Arlene's mind.

"Nice greeting. Lovely place here, Arlene. Let me grab my bag." I handed her the flowers.

"Come on in. You need a hand with anything?"

"No, I'm good. I have this one bag and a couple of bottles of wine. I thought you drank white, so I got one Pinot Grigio and one Sauvignon Blanc."

"Both are perfect. You must be exhausted. What can I get you?"

"Nothing just yet. Your place is adorable. Is this all your own artwork?"

"Most of it. I bought a couple of pieces from friends. Let me give you a quick tour; it doesn't take long. It's only a two bedroom, but it works for me."

The house was small but was lovely, colorful, tasteful and I think you'd call it comfy. The kitchen was a good size and she remodeled with expensive sub-zero appliances and cookery. I recalled Arlene mentioning she loved to cook.

No matter how hard I tried, I could not detect any cat smell. I wonder if she had it fumigated before or after I called.

When we got to her bedroom, she suggested I put my bag down.

"I hope you will not hate me, but do you remember Connie Zucker from the neighborhood?"

"Sure."

"She lives up in Pompano, only twenty minutes from here, and when I told her you were visiting, she insisted we have dinner. She reserved for seven at Shooters over on the Inter-Coastal. I hope that's OK."

"Relax, Arlene. That's fine; it will be nice to see Connie. I could use, in this order, a shower, a power nap, and a drink. I'll try to stay awake through dinner."

"Sure. I left extra towels in the bathroom; if you need anything, holler. Frank, I am excited to have you here. I'm glad you thought of staying here."

"My favorite person in Florida; who else would I ask? But I appreciate you're having me. They said they would have my place done in two days, three at the most. And today is one of them."

"You're welcome as long as you want. Now, go get your shower and nap."

"Yes, ma'am."

I got a quick shower, set my Fitbit alarm for five-forty-five, and stretched out for a nap.

I was quite certain I slept, but at five-twenty-five, I felt a hand stroking my Mr. Happy. "Did you know you snore?"

"Only when I sense I am being attacked in bed," rolling over to confront a naked Arlene. "Oh my, so you're napping also?"

"I just thought maybe you'd like some company."

"You would be correct, Arlene," I said while returning her strokes and kissing her with all I had.

She took off my tee shirt while I wiggled out of my shorts. There was a second's hesitation while we each tried to decide who was mounting whom. She answered that question.

"Do you know how long I thought about this, Frank?" I wasn't certain I could have a casual conversation at that moment. I think Jerry and Elaine did that, but this is real life. "Twenty years?" I replied, thinking it may have been since our last make-out session, and not yesterday's phone call.

"Since we were sixteen." I left that matzoh ball hanging there while I stayed focused on the job at hand. Both of us were now panting and moaning, and it would be a close call at the finish line. I think it was a photo finish, as I collapsed, and she screamed.

We remain entwined in each other's sweat, nibbling at our ears, stroking each other, and kissing.

"I hate to be a spoil-sort, Ar, but I'm going to need another shower. You might too. Let's go."

By six-fifteen, she joined me at her kitchen counter, where I had a glass of wine waiting for her, and a vodka for me.

"Wow, you look great, Arlene." And she did in a yellow sleeveless tank top with spaghetti strap, a low, scoop neck sexy casual look. White capris, yellow and white sandals, bangle bracelets, diamond studs, and a gold choker completed the outfit.

I would change, but I brought nothing dressier. I wore tan shorts and a yellow and blue checked dress shirt I wore with the tail out.

"You look great yourself, Frank," picking up her glass and offering a toast. "To our afternoon delight, and the end of sixty years of delayed gratification."

"I think we caught up rather quickly." She put her wineglass down and put her arms around my neck. "It was worth the wait, but let's not wait so long for the next time."

I looked at my watch and said, "I'm counting the minutes."

Chapter 53

Juanita White agreed to meet for lunch with Chad Winters at Hudson's, another landmark restaurant on Skull Creek. Winters thought if it was not too cold, they could sit outside and have more privacy.

They were lucky, as it was sixty-five degrees, and at eleven-forty-five, they had their choice of tables. They had no trouble meeting up, and Butch Weir introduced himself and Winters.

"Thank you for meeting with us, Ms. White."

"Please call me Juanita, and I'm not certain one can turn down a meeting request from SLED. I'm anxious to hear what this is about."

"Why don't we look at menus and order first?" Weir suggested.

They did, and all ordered cups of She Crab soup and shrimp Po Boys. *You don't come to Hudson's and order burgers.*

"OK, let's hear it," White said as soon as the server withdrew.

"Sure. Can you tell us how well you know Alan Baxter?"

White hesitated, not expecting that question. Not knowing what they knew, she was not about to say too much.

"Not very well. Major Baxter occasionally attends Town Council meetings, so, yes, I have met him."

"That's it? You never saw him outside of meetings? Do you do any business with him?" Weir persisted.

A bit more concerned, she replied, "We may have attended a social gathering or two in our official capacities, but I am not in business and have none with the major."

Weir hesitated as the server approached and set down their soups.

"Juanita, I'll ask you one more time, and please take your time in answering. Have you ever been on Major Baxter's boat?"

Oh mercy me, White thought to herself. "Do I need an attorney?"

"You tell me, Juanita. Let me tell you what we know. We know Baxter is a drug lord, and he delivers drugs by boat to dealers up and down the coast. We know some of these dealers, and we have pictures of you on his boat.

"Baxter is also our primary suspect in at least one murder. We are eager to learn of your role in the Baxter Enterprise, Juanita."

Knowing that the gig was up, White took a deep breath. "After my husband died, money was tight. I don't know how Baxter knew this, or if he did, but he visited with me and said he could help, and all I would need to do was, occasionally, support his agenda in the Town Council. He said I would most likely support these positions anyway, and for the most part, this was true.

"For the first couple of years, I did not know what Baxter's motive was, but I heard on the grapevine that he was involved in drugs. I didn't understand how our Town Council policies played into that, but then it became clear he wanted less of a police presence along the coast and at Coligny Beach."

"And why did you visit his boat at night?"

"He asked me to come by at night to pick up something, meaning an envelope with payment. In hindsight, I think it had more to do with digging his hook further into me. He now had witnesses to my visiting him, and I could not withdraw from our arrangement. I swear, this was my only involvement; a couple of votes here and there."

Their server delivered their sandwiches and asked if we needed anything else.

"Are you aware of any other council members doing the same?"

"I am not, but I would find it surprising if I were the only one."

"Juanita, we need you to come to Charleston in the next day or two and give a statement. We will read your rights to you and discuss possible charges against you. I would suggest bringing an attorney. It goes without saying, do not think about calling Baxter or mentioning this to anyone other than your attorney and close family.

"With the other evidence we have and other witness statements, we've got enough on Baxter for an arrest. Call me as soon as you can to let me know when you come to Charleston."

"What am I looking at here, Mr. Weir?"

"The County Attorney will decide that, Juanita. It will be difficult for her to ignore the bribery charges, but with your cooperation, we will ask her to ignore or go easy on the drug trafficking."

White had lost her appetite and was sobbing. Weir and Winters finished their sandwiches, and Weir paid the check.

They walked out to the parking lot together. "I'm sorry it came to this, Juanita, but we cannot sweep the misdeeds of public officials under the carpet. Please call me by tomorrow."

"I will, and I'm sorry too, for everything."

Weir wondered if she regretted taking bribes, or getting caught taking bribes. He thought she meant it, though.

Chapter 54

PHILADELPHIA INQUIRER, JANUARY 29, 2025
ICE CONFIRMS RAID & ARRESTS IN PHILLY HUMAN TRAFFICKING RING!

A spokesperson for The Philadelphia Office of the Immigration and Customs Enforcement (ICE) confirmed yesterday they made a series of arrests in a Philadelphia-based Human Trafficking and Prostitution syndicate.

Cooperating with the Philadelphia Police Department, ICE raided a home in the 2200 block of North Broad Street at three o'clock yesterday afternoon. They arrested seven people, including two Serbian Nationals, who appeared to be the leaders at this location.

The officers also took twenty-one women into custody. They believe the Serbs brought the women into this country under the pretext of good jobs and housing but instead, held them captive and forced them into prostitution. All of them had forged immigration documents.

It is unclear what charges authorities may file against the women.

>In separate raids, ICE arrested Sean O'Connor, Jr. of The O'Connor Group, and Eli Kapustin, David Kapustin, and Myra Feldman of ELK Advisors, and charged them with Human Trafficking, Prostitution, Racketeering, and Money Laundering.
>
>The O'Connor Group is a large accounting, investment, and insurance advisory firm founded in 1978 by Sean P. O'Connor.
>
>ELK Advisors is a private investment and consulting firm working only with wealthy clients.
>
>The syndicate came to the attention of the Philadelphia police when they were investigating the murder of Sean O'Connor, Sr. An unknown suspect murdered O'Connor on December 10th on the St. Joseph University campus. Authorities do not believe there is a connection between the crime operation and the death of O'Connor. The Philadelphia Police are still investigating potential suspects.
>
>The spokesperson said they expected to make more arrests in the coming days.

Vernon Brown, Roberta Rumson, and Captain Eleanor Webster sat in the captain's office.

"At least we got mentioned, if not any personal glory. I guess that's something," Webster said.

"I guess so, and I suspect this was the tip of that iceberg. I think there are more girls from different countries, and O'Connor and Kapustin are all over that," Brown added.

"Hey, before I forget, the Commissioner wants to know who the hell killed Sean O'Connor?"

The three officers looked at each other, shrugged, and smiled.

The next few days were a blur for me.

We had dinner with Connie Zucker Gold and her husband, Simon.

We spent the next two days at the beach; one with a couple of Arlene's local friends, and one day with two women from high school that we both knew.

In between, Arlene and I continued enjoying each other. As great as this was, I was getting antsy to get back to Hilton Head. I spoke with Chad Winters this morning and, while offering no details, he said arrests were close and he thought it safe for me to return home.

Over coffee, I asked Arlene, "Any plans tonight?"

"No, I thought I would cook. I made you suffer enough with all the socializing.

"How about just you and I going out for dinner? I got a text message this morning, and they finished with the repairs on the apartment, so I'm going to take off in the morning."

"Already? It seems like you just got here."

"I know, but I feel like I have interrupted your life. You have friends and a business. You don't need me taking up your time."

"Frank, I love having you here. Promise me you'll come back soon."

"I promise. How about Burlock Coast in the Ritz? I've heard good things about it."

"Never been there, but you're right. It's supposed to be very nice. I'll make a reservation."

"Already done."

"Quite presumptuous of you."

"Not presumptuous, optimistic."

Arlene and I both dressed in our best for our last meal. Of course, it meant the same shorts and dress shirt I wore at Donna's. Arlene was in a long, powder blue sleeveless sundress with a slit on the side.

"Do you always need to look so much better than me, Arlene? It's getting embarrassing."

"Thank you, but you look great yourself. I'm ready."

It was a twenty-minute drive into the Fort Lauderdale beach area. I gave the car to the valet. The hostess showed us to a table by a window that overlooked the Ritz-Carlton pool and, in the distance, the beach and ocean.

Drinks, dinner, conversation, and people-watching were all wonderful, and we were both exhausted by the time we got back to her house. I took advantage of my last time to seduce Arlene, at least on this trip.

I was up early the next morning and showered, dressed, and finished packing as quietly as I could so as not to wake her. It almost worked.

"You would not leave without saying goodbye, were you?"

"Of course not. I was going to give you another five minutes."

"Go get some coffee, and I'll be right out."

She came out five minutes later, and I had coffee waiting for her. She joined me at the counter. After taking her first sip, she said, "I've never been to Hilton Head. How about if I come up and visit for a few days?"

"I'd love that, Ar. Let me check my schedule when I get back. I have a couple of things going on," like trying not to get killed, "and I'll let you know. Remember, it's about twenty degrees colder up there."

"I'm sure I can stand it, and I'll have you to keep me warm."

"I'll do my best."

We finished coffee, and I was out the door on schedule at seven-thirty-five. I had several stops at places that were not on the Island, Trader Joe's, Wawa, and Buc-ees. With the stops, it would be another nine hours in the saddle. I hoped my back and bladder were up to the challenge.

Two hours into the drive, I had a text message from Arlene, *MISS YOU.*

At five-forty, I pulled to my parking garage, exhausted, but thinking I had a good week in Florida and enjoyed Donna and Arlene.

One or both qualified for further consideration.

The only downside of the trip was that I exhausted my supply of Tadalafil.

Chapter 56

Juanita White did her part.

She brought her attorney to Charleston and gave a full statement, including the payments she received, dates she had met with Baxter, and the names of Baxter's friends she could remember.

Besides Weir, Winters, and Flores, SLED's District Attorney, Geraldine DeLoach, was in the meeting. She told them she had discussed the case with the governor, and they would be as lenient as the law allowed. That meant as little as sixty days' jail time, fines, probation, and prohibition from public office.

This morning, White called Winters and said she received an email from Baxter. He was having friends on his boat, *THE MAJOR'S MARINER,* for drinks and fellowship from eight until eleven tonight. Baxter would dock the boat at Pawley's Island south parking lot.

She told them this was how Baxter advised his group that a drug shipment had been delivered and could be picked up. There would be drinks and food, but also exchanges of drugs and cash.

Winters called Weir, and they began putting in motion the raid, planning to hit the boat by land and sea. They would have a SWAT team approach by land, and a Coast Guard team on the water prepared to intercept any boats trying to flee.

White had emailed Baxter that she could not attend, as she had plans with friends to see *Jersey Boys* at the Arts Center.

Weir and Winters discussed the logistical challenge of planning an operation in the winter in this desolate section of Pawley's Island. At any other time, the owners and tourists occupied the homes and The Last Resort, a zero-star motel, but most sat empty in the winter.

Cookie Flores spoke with Pawleys Island Police Chief Michael Fogarty, who told her The Last Resort was open, and he'd drive over to speak with Jake Sharpton, the owner.

By four-thirty that afternoon, they had the makings of a plan. A SLED SWAT team was en route to the police station in Georgetown, South Carolina, about fifteen minutes from The Last Resort. Weir, Winters, and Flores would meet them there at six. The Coast Guard would have two cutters in Pawley's Inlet, out of sight of The Last Resort.

The Georgetown Police would have two ambulances, and a team of officers depart for the dock to provide support for any injuries and arrest the suspects.

At seven o'clock, the SWAT teams would go to The Last Resort in two vans, a white one marked Lowcountry Heating and Plumbing, and a black one marked Carter's Construction & Home Remodeling.

They all synced their watches, and Weir designated nine o'clock as GO TIME. All had earpieces in their helmets and Weir and SWAT team Leader Michaels had microphones.

Food and coffee were available as the teams tried to relax.

Michaels asked Weir, "What are we expecting here, Butch?"

"I can't be sure, Ed. There could be ten to twenty people on Baxter's boat. They are drug dealers, so they all could be armed. I wish I could tell you if they will resist or surrender, but we must be prepared for them to resist.

"Our advantage will be that your people can spread out as they approach the dock, but they'll all be in one place. Once we start moving, the Coast Guard cutters will come out and block any of the boats, and then move in from the rear."

"You're making it sound too easy."

"What did that boxer say? *Your game plan is great until you get hit in the jaw.*"

At six-forty-five, they all took their the last toilet breaks, and triple-checked their communications. The SWAT team loaded into the vans and pulled out.

At seven-fifteen, Weir, Winters, Flores, and two SWAT team members drove to an area that would give them cover but also allow them to view the dock.

Nothing to do now but wait. Law enforcement officers always claimed they spent more time waiting than anything else. At least no one was alone, and they could make small talk to ease the tension. But Butch Weir didn't do this often anymore, and he was antsy.

At seven-thirty-five, Baxter's boat eased into the dock and moored. Weir was relieved no one had warned Baxter, and he didn't call off this rendezvous. Weir updated the SWAT and Coast Guard teams.

Weir could see Baxter on board with three other men. Baxter was at the helm with night vision binoculars, searching the area for anything that did not belong. A couple of lights were on at The Last Resort, but there was nothing unusual about that.

A second boat moored at seven-fifty-five, and two men went aboard *The Major's Mariner*. Over the next half hour, four more boats arrived, each with two or three men. Weir had counted seventeen people, including two women on board the Mariner.

At ten minutes before nine, Weir cleared the Coast Guard to move into position, blocking the harbor.

When the Coast Guard communicated they were in position, Weir gave the go call at nine o'clock. His team began walking towards the dock while the SWAT team at The Last Resort exited one by one, spreading out as they started inching forward.

When Weir's team was within fifty yards of the dock, a voice came over a loudspeaker, "Halt right there. This is the owner of The Major's Mariner. This is a private party, so please leave this area now."

"Major Baxter, this is Major Weir of SLED's NAV Division. We are coming aboard, major."

"I think not. While there is alcohol on board, there are no narcotics, so please remove yourselves now."

"That not going to happen, major. Please stand down."

With that, Weir resumed their approach to the dock. There was a gunshot. The five of them ducked under the tall seagrass, but there was no other shelter. So much for the peaceful surrender.

"That was a warning shot, major. We are armed and prepared to defend our position. This is the last warning."

Remaining hidden by the grass, Weir broadcasted, "And this is your warning, major. You are under arrest. You have the right to remain silent. Anything you do say may be used against you. You have the right to have an attorney present during questioning now or in the future. If you decide to answer any questions now, without an attorney present...

"I know my rights, major. And I know there is a law against unlawful search and seizure, and our right to bear arms."

"We have a warrant for your arrest, and to search the premises. We are now coming on board."

With that, there were two shots fired into the grass, close enough for Weir to realize they could not wait for a peaceful resolution. Into his walkie-talkie, Weir said, "Ed, you can hear me?"

"Copy, major."

"Time for us to send a warning of our own. Fire a barrage into the side of the boat. Do not aim to kill anyone. Copy?"

"Copy, major."

Weir asked the Coast Guard to move in with caution.

In rapid order, the SWAT fired twenty-five rounds into the side of The Major's Mariner. Five men jumped off the Mariner and jumped into two separate boats.

Five more shots came into the high grass, one hitting Winters in the shoulder.

Weir spoke into his mike, "We've got one wounded; send ambulances. There will be more. Ed, send another twenty rounds aiming at anyone you see with a weapon. Coast Guard, move in with full sirens. Let's let them know we ain't backing off."

There were thirty seconds of back-and-forth gunfire but then silence, as the SWAT team was now twenty-five yards from the Mariner. Weir's team joined them. The Coast Guard cutters were fifty yards behind them.

Weir used the megaphone. "All of you not named Baxter need to decide now. We are prepared to sink that boat and all of you with it. Baxter wants to play macho man and take y'all with him. It's your call."

It remained quiet, as they no doubt were considering their options. None were good, but only one kept them alive.

"We're out," was yelled as a man and a woman stepped off the boat, throwing their weapons down and holding their hands over their heads.

With these two surrenders, others followed them, and one by one, they walked off the boat with their hands held over their heads.

Weir called Georgetown for the ambulance and police to join them for the clean-up. Only Winters suffered a wound on their team, and only a minor one. But according to Weir's count, there were four from the boat, including Baxter, unaccounted for.

"What are you thinking, Baxter?"

"I've got three wounded here, one pretty seriously. I'll come out first, then you can help them."

Baxter walked off with his hands up and head down. He said nothing as the police handcuffed him and placed him in the prisoner's van. The medics quickly moved onto the boat to deal with the three wounded. They were all taken to the Beaufort Memorial Hospital. Winters chose not to go to the hospital and had his wound treated by the EMT at the station.

It would be a long night for all involved, reports, bookings, mugshots and fingerprints, and evidence gathering on the boats.

Officials later reported later it was the largest drug bust ever in the Lowcountry. Everyone learned of Major Alan Baxter's jaded history, and his ill-fated, influence-pedaled rise through the ranks of the Beaufort County Sheriff's Office.

At four the next morning, Chad Winters was home and ready to get a few hours' sleep. But not before sending one last text message:

MR. LAZARUS...IT'S OVER! IT IS SAFE FOR YOU TO RETURN HOME. I'LL CALL YOU SOON. CHAD WINTERS, SLED, NAV.

Chapter 57

Two weeks after the raid on Broad Street, and the arrests of Sean O'Connor, Jr. and the Kapustins, Vernon Brown and James McNeil were having coffee and donuts at their usual Dunkin at Fifty-second and Chestnut Streets.

James asked, "Anyone get killed this morning, Vern?"

"Not yet, brother James, but it's still early, plenty of time."

"Any recent developments in the O'Connor case?"

"Oh, ICE is having a great time. Their dealmaking with their captors yielded them three new cells with Asian, black, and Swedish girls, all under the O'Connor and Kapustin umbrella.

"Kapustin continues to claim he was just paying bills, and O'Connor said he was only screwing the girls and did not know his dad was behind it.

"But we are no closer to finding the senior's murderer. We interviewed all current and former employees twice. A couple of names given to us by the local bangers yielded nada; we are at square one."

"It's over two months now, Vern. Is it officially a cold-case?"

"If no leads develop in the next week or two, it will be. Hey, how would you like to take a long weekend trip down to Hilton Head?"

"What's on Hilton Head?"

"I thought I told you; we caught a license plate at the time of the murder and the driver worked for O'Connor thirty-five years ago. His name is Lazarus, like Jesus' buddy. We interviewed twice over the phone, and the captain would not allow a trip down there.

"I'd have to take a day or two off and pay for the trip, but something about the guy was off. He kept insisting he created me in a novel he wrote."

"Dude will cop an insanity plea, Vern, but I'm up for a trip, subject to Linda's approval."

"That goes without saying. Let's shoot for next weekend."

"You mean this weekend? This weekend is the next weekend."

"If I meant this weekend, I would have said this weekend. Next weekend, James."

"Got it."

***

With the Captain's and wives' approvals, Vern and James made their plans. The wives' approvals were contingent on all four taking a vacation on Hilton Head when the weather was warmer.

The American Airlines flight left Philadelphia at ten-ten on Friday morning and arrived at Hilton Head airport at eleven-fifty-five.

They carried their bags and had a rental car by twelve-thirty. They were staying at the Westin Hilton, ten minutes from the airport. They splurged as they were told the February rates were half of what they would be in July and August.

They found the hotel in Port Royal Plantation. Formerly, many of the subdivisions on Hilton Head were called "Plantations," but in keeping with the times, many had dropped the controversial word. Others still refused to acquiesce to wokeness.

After checking in, unpacking, and texting their wives, James said, "Why not grab a quick lunch, and then see if we can connect with your perp?"

"Makes sense. We passed Crazy Crab on the way in and that was one of ten restaurants suggested to me."

They drove five minutes to the restaurant, which was less than half full on a winter afternoon.

Brown ordered a Caesar Salad with grilled salmon, and McNeil the blackened Mahi-Mahi sandwich. They each had a Michelob Ultra.

James could tell his friend was preoccupied and eager to confront this Lazarus guy, so they ate quietly and quickly. Forty-five minutes later, they were back in the car and headed down the island to Shelter Cove. Forty-Seven Shelter Cove Lane was the WaterWalk apartment complex on the bank of the Broad Creek that divided the island into east and west.

They pulled into a parking spot in front of the office.

Pulling out his badge, Brown approached the concierge and said, "We are here to see Frank Lazarus. How do we enter the building?"

Looking at Brown's badge, Samantha Wilson asked, "Philadelphia Po-Leece? Is Mr. Lazarus expecting you?"

"I doubt it."

"Have you called him?"

"No."

"Residents admit their visitors using the touchpad on the side of the building which calls them, and they can buzz them in on their phone. You or I could call Mr. Lazarus, and if he's there, I'm sure he'll come down to let you in."

"Would you please try? Thank you."

Wilson looked up the phone number and dialed. Getting no answer, she left a message. "Hey, Frank, this is Samantha in the office. Please call me when you get this message. Thank you."

"He might be in his apartment but not answering the phone, or he could be anywhere. We do not keep track of the comings and goings of our residents."

When I came off the 18th green at four-thirty, I saw I had two messages. One from the apartment's office, and the other from Detective Brown. *Were they related? Is it possible Brown is here? Did he find something? Impossible!*

I called Samantha first, and she confirmed Brown was indeed on the Island. Will, Scott, and Tom were waiting for me in the lounge. Brown could wait.

At five-forty-five, I returned Brown's call. "Mr. Lazarus. This is Detective Brown of the Philly PD. Thanks for returning my call."

"You're welcome, I'm sure. What's up?"

"James McNeil and I are on Hilton Head and hoped to visit with you. Can we see you tonight?"

"James is with you? That's exciting, but I'm sorry, I'm out with friends for dinner. Can this wait until tomorrow? I can see you in the morning."

" I guess so. Would ten o'clock be OK?"

"Sure. Do you know where I live?"

"Yes, but how do we get into the building?"

"Go to the keypad on the door to the right of the office. Enter 217. It should ring my cellphone, and I'll buzz you in. It's a very efficient system that works almost 50% of the time. Then take the elevator to the second floor. I'll meet you there. And James is coming with you? I am excited to meet him."

"He'll be with me. I'll see you in the morning."

Shit! This would keep me awake tonight, even though I know I'll just deny anything he throws at me. Even though it will be neat to meet James McNeil.

Chapter 58

I was up early the next morning, anticipating a visit from my two favorite characters, Detective Vernon Brown and James McNeil.

I drove to Island Deli and picked up a half dozen assorted bagels.

Am I a great host, or what?

Despite the chilly forty-five-degree temperature this morning, forecasters predicted it to reach sixty degrees. I wore shorts and my Overbrook sweatshirt, remembering those two were from West Philly High, Overbrook's hated rival.

At five before ten, my phone rang. They had navigated our confusing entry system. I pushed the ENTER button, buzzing the door open. I walked out to the elevator to meet them.

As the elevator door opened, I said, "You found me. Good morning, gentlemen. This is a real thrill for me."

I led them back to my apartment.

"Can I offer you coffee or tea?" even though I was not sure I had tea. At Dunkin, I always had them drinking coffee.

"Sure, black for me," Brown answered.

"Same for me, thank you."

"Help yourselves to bagels. I thought about getting donuts at Dunkin, but remembered you get enough of them back in Philly. James, did Vernon tell you this very eerie story we have?"

"You mean the one about you creating us? He did. I agree, very eerie."

Still standing, Brown said, "You have a lovely view here. What's the water out there?"

"That's the Broad Creek. You're lucky it's high tide. At low tide, you can't even see water. Have a seat." I ushered them towards the living room with their coffees.

"How long have you been here?" Brown asked.

"The better part of nine years. The last six here and before that, I was off the island.

"What brings you to the Island, business or pleasure?"

"You."

"I'm flattered. So, what's on your mind?"

"I know you killed Sean O'Connor, but why?"

"I'm sorry, Vernon, but the WHY is your answer. Why would I kill Sean O'Connor? I have not seen the man in twenty years and haven't worked with him for thirty. I am happily retired down here, making only an annual trek up to Philly to see friends and family. You must have had many people with much greater motives. I don't own a gun and haven't fired a weapon since 1966 in the Army's Basic Training."

"But you were at the basketball game the night of his murder and parked on Cardinal Avenue."

"Whether or not you believe in them, Vernon, coincidences do occur. You've asked that question twice now and my answer remains the same. I am a St. Joe alum, and I attend a basketball game or two when I'm in Philly if the schedule works for me. How would I know Sean would be at the game that night?"

"And how about your meeting with Mr. Talarico twelve months before that, and asking about O'Connor?"

"I can assure you there was nothing nefarious about that. I was having dinner with an old friend and asking about the only person we had in common, and Jamie's boss." Standing, I asked, "A second cup for anyone?"

They both declined, but I got myself one, giving Brown time to regroup. As I returned, "James, are you still doing your gig at The Jazz Corner in Philly?"

"We are, every Thursday night."

"Here's another coincidence for you, Vernon. We also have a Jazz Corner on Hilton Head, you came by it on the way on to the Island. And James, now that I know you are a real person, perhaps I'll stop in the next time I'm in Philly."

"Please do."

"Anything else I can answer for you, Vernon?"

"I know you did it, but I don't know yet how to prove it."

"Vernon, you came up empty on current and past employees, O'Connor's girlfriends and prostitutes, Serbian human traffickers, and West Philly gang-bangers. Now you decide a seventy-eight-year-old former employee of thirty years ago must be the doer? Where is that detective who was so intuitive in *CLAUDIA'S REVENGE*?"

"James, it appears we have gotten everything we will out of Mr. Lazarus. You ready?"

"You do not need to go so soon, do you? I thought we might discuss my next novel. I have been thinking that you and your wives could vacation here on Hilton Head, and a murder takes place while you're here. You get involved in the search for the killer. Like it?"

Brown did not answer, but James said, "I've got a list of suggested restaurants here. Care to give me your thoughts?" handing me his phone.

"Let's see. You're from Philly. You are not going Italian down here, even though Michael Anthony, Ombra, and Nunzio's all have their roots in Philly. That leaves you Hudson's or Poseidon for seafood, Crane's or Bowdie's for steaks, and One Hot Mama's for barbecue. That should keep you busy. If Vernon comes to his senses, I'd love to join you. I have so many questions for you both. James, how is Claudia doing?"

"She's recovering. Thanks for asking, Frank."

Vernon Brown stood and waited for James McNeil to do so.

Walking towards the door, Brown said, "Thanks for the coffee and your time, Frank. I'll be back in touch."

"Any time, Vernon. And call me for dinner. Great meeting you, James."

"Same here, Frank."

As soon as the door closed, Vernon said to James, "The man is a fucking psychopath."

"I liked the guy. Have you considered he might be innocent?"

"No!"

The End

AUTHOR'S NOTES

When I first thought about this concept, I must admit I wasn't certain it would work. I hope you'll write to me one way or the other with your answer.

I had to convince my significant other, Deb, she had to be left out of the story. I needed a love interest on Hilton Head to get murdered, and my trip to Florida to hide from Major Baxter.

I asked her if she would prefer to get killed, but she approved of her omission.

But there are real friends and family mentioned, and Vernon Brown, James McNeil, Roberta Rumson, Heem Jones, Charles Bishop, Harvey Green, David Kasper, and Michelle Pugh all reprised their roles from *The Murder Gambit, The Phenom, and the April Fools duology*.

As always, I must thank Deb for her contributions and patience. She has a tough job.

Once again, my thanks go out to proofreader and editor extraordinaire, Charles Senna.

I hope you have enjoyed this story, and I thank you so much for buying it. If you would be kind enough to leave a positive review on Goodreads or the site where you bought the book, I would sincerely appreciate it. Reviews matter to independent authors like me.

I'd love to hear from you; write to me at FrankLazScribe@gmail.com.

Sign-up for my Newsletter and FREE eBook at http://eepurl.com/iqUjbQ

Follow me on Social Media at https://linktr.ee/franklaz

Or visit my website at https://franklazscribe.com

All the Best!

Frank Lazarus